A blanket of silence
fell over the crowd

The sword was raised slowly. It descended in a wide arc, flashing in the morning sun, and sliced cleanly through flesh and bone. The guards were mesmerized.

Bolan went into action, kicking the nearest guard and snatching his M-16 in one fluid movement. He switched to full-auto and sprayed a burst above the heads of the men who rushed him.

His only chance of escape lay in the twisted alleyways of the souks. The Executioner was on the run. God help anyone who tried to stop him.

MACK BOLAN®

The Executioner

#60 Sold for Slaughter
#61 Tiger War
#62 Day of Mourning
#63 The New War Book
#64 Dead Man Running
#65 Cambodia Clash
#66 Orbiting Omega
#67 Beirut Payback
#68 Prairie Fire
#69 Skysweeper
#70 Ice Cold Kill
#71 Blood Dues
#72 Hellbinder
#73 Appointment in Kabul
#74 Savannah Swingsaw
#75 The Bone Yard
#76 Teheran Wipeout
#77 Hollywood Hell
#78 Death Games
#79 Council of Kings
#80 Running Hot
#81 Shock Waves
#82 Hammerhead Reef
#83 Missouri Deathwatch
#84 Fastburn
#85 Sunscream
#86 Hell's Gate
#87 Hellfire Crusade
#88 Baltimore Trackdown
#89 Defenders and Believers
#90 Blood Heat Zero
#91 The Trial
#92 Moscow Massacre
#93 The Fire Eaters
#94 Save the Children
#95 Blood and Thunder
#96 Death Has a Name
#97 Meltdown
#98 Black Dice
#99 Code of Dishonor

#100 Blood Testament
#101 Eternal Triangle
#102 Split Image
#103 Assault on Rome
#104 Devil's Horn
#105 Countdown to Chaos
#106 Run to Ground
#107 American Nightmare
#108 Time to Kill
#109 Hong Kong Hit List
#110 Trojan Horse
#111 The Fiery Cross
#112 Blood of the Lion
#113 Vietnam Fallout
#114 Cold Judgment
#115 Circle of Steel
#116 The Killing Urge
#117 Vendetta in Venice
#118 Warrior's Revenge
#119 Line of Fire
#120 Border Sweep
#121 Twisted Path
#122 Desert Strike

Stony Man Doctrine
Terminal Velocity
Resurrection Day
Dirty War
Flight 741
Dead Easy
Sudden Death
Rogue Force
Tropic Heat
Fire in the Sky
Anvil of Hell
Flash Point
Flesh and Blood
Moving Target

DON PENDLETON's EXECUTIONER
MACK BOLAN.

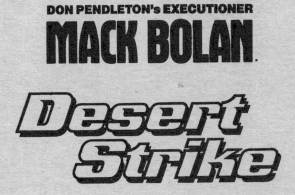

Desert Strike

A GOLD EAGLE BOOK FROM
WORLDWIDE.

TORONTO • NEW YORK • LONDON • PARIS
AMSTERDAM • STOCKHOLM • HAMBURG
ATHENS • MILAN • TOKYO • SYDNEY

First edition February 1989

ISBN 0-373-61122-6

Special thanks and acknowledgment to
Jack Garside for his contribution to this work.

Although the force of fanatical passion is far greater than that exerted by any philosophical belief, its sanction is just the same. It gives men something which they think is sublime to fight for, and this serves them as an excuse for wars...

—Winston Churchill
The River War

A fanatic has no choice but to lose his objectivity—and very soon after, his freedom and innocence. We all need something to believe in. Let's just inject it with a dose of reality.

—Mack Bolan

THE
MACK BOLAN®
LEGEND

Nothing less than a war could have fashioned the destiny of the man called Mack Bolan. Bolan earned the Executioner title in the jungle hell of Vietnam.

But this soldier also wore another name—Sergeant Mercy. He was so tagged because of the compassion he showed to wounded comrades-in-arms and Vietnamese civilians.

Mack Bolan's second tour of duty ended prematurely when he was given emergency leave to return home and bury his family, victims of the Mob. Then he declared a one-man war against the Mafia.

He confronted the Families head-on from coast to coast, and soon a hope of victory began to appear. But Bolan had broken society's every rule. That same society started gunning for this elusive warrior—to no avail.

So Bolan was offered amnesty to work within the system against terrorism. This time, as an employee of Uncle Sam, Bolan became Colonel John Phoenix. With a command center at Stony Man Farm in Virginia, he and his new allies—Able Team and Phoenix Force—waged relentless war on a new adversary: the KGB.

But when his one true love, April Rose, died at the hands of the Soviet terror machine, Bolan severed all ties with Establishment authority.

Now, after a lengthy lone-wolf struggle and much soul-searching, the Executioner has agreed to enter an ''arm's-length'' alliance with his government once more, reserving the right to pursue personal missions in his Everlasting War.

PROLOGUE

The king stood at the balustrade, a solitary man with a short, round body, his plump cheeks framed by a flowing white *guttra*. A wistful smile spread across his kindly face as he looked down from his palace, a luxurious eagle's nest built on the crest of the mountains. Thousands of feet below, the Plain of Hejaz stretched from horizon to horizon. In the distance the Red Sea was a blue haze dotted by scores of dhows, whose owners were plying their trade up and down the coast as they had for thousands of years.

The king imagined he could see Mecca far off to his right. On a clear day, and with binoculars, he could see the top of Mount Arafat. The Great Mosque, the Holy Mosque of the Kabah and the center of his universe, was hidden by a ridge of hills. He was a religious man and at that moment his thoughts were on the paradox of his life—his wish to spend his time peacefully with the scholars of Islam, the ulema—and the fact that his duty was to head a family envied by many and constantly targeted for death.

"It is time," his brother Mansur said, coming up behind him. He was a tall man who towered above his older brother. "Even kings do not keep the ulema waiting."

The king smiled at his favorite brother as he moved off along the balcony to the waiting cars.

As usual, six cars were lined up in front of the palace. The first two and the last two were for national guardsmen. One was for the king and his brothers, one for their close attendants—six white stretch Mercedes worth more than a million dollars.

A third brother, Turki, had been chatting with the captain of the guard. "You look tired, brother," he said, addressing the king. Within the family, titles were never used, but respect was evident. "Must you go to Mecca today?"

"Yes, I must go. The ulema wish me to see the new covering they have made for the Holy Kabah, the house of Abraham. Examining their work is not a chore, Turki. I consider it a great honor. The hajj will be upon us in a matter of days, and pilgrims will arrive from all over the world. We must play our part."

The group of limousines was always preceded by four army sergeants on motorcycles, and a weapons carrier holding four national guardsmen always brought up the rear. In case of an attack the front and rear cars were to crash into the attaching vehicles. The second and fifth cars were to pull up alongside the royal cars, forming a buffer against enemy fire. The weapons carrier and the cyclists had free rein to move where needed. The entourage looked efficient as it moved off, but this day was like any other for the troops. It was just another boring assignment.

As they started down the newly opened highway, the king's thoughts were on the miracle wrought by the imagination and fortitude of his brother, King Faisal, and on the house of al-Ghosaibi. Almost twenty years ago the al-Ghosaibi patriarch had conceived the miracle highway that now connected the winter capital of Taif with the plains and cities below. Faisal had found the funds for road construction before oil money was plentiful, and he had pushed for completion.

Both men were dead. During construction, al-Ghosaíbi's plane had crashed against the towering rock on one of his daily inspections. Soon after, Faisal had been assassinated by a power-mad nephew. They had gone to Paradise without seeing the miracle they had started. The winding highway snaked its way left and right, descending ten thousand feet in barely a half-hour drive. It was one of the new wonders of the world.

Now the highway was so vital to the commerce of the kingdom that to halt traffic for the passage of the king would be unthinkable. Since truckers no longer had to drive hundreds of miles out of their way to scale the mountains, the highway was always crowded. Several heavily laden Mercedes trucks lumbered behind the cavalcade as the royal vehicles started into the first turn. Five or six more were approaching from the turn below.

The action happened very quickly—too quickly for military minds dulled by routine to react. Four huge trucks behind the cavalcade increased speed, crowding the weapons carrier. Soldiers on the carrier waved them off. They couldn't conceive that it was an attack—it was the usual madness of Bedouin truckers.

The lead truck pulled out swiftly on the steep descent and with its tremendous bulk, easily nosed the weapons carrier over the edge.

Not one shot was fired.

The four trucks moved alongside. As the two streams of vehicles headed downward, cars heading up the two-lane road took to the shoulder and managed to squeeze by. Larger vehicles crawled partway up the loose shale of the mountain wall to avoid the rogue trucks, and as the slope steepened they tipped over. The four behemoths continued to hog the road.

The frantic limousine drivers tried to speed up but were trapped behind slow-moving trucks. Weapons were almost useless in the hands of petrified guards as the trucks towered over them. With shaking hands they fumbled open electric windows and switched their submachine guns to full-auto. But one look at the towering vehicles told them they had little hope of hitting anything.

Slowly and relentlessly, the four giant vehicles eased closer to the expensive cars. One by one they pushed them over the edge of the mountains, the roar of their engines drowning out the screams of the men inside.

The weapons carrier had strewn its bloodied cargo over the craggy outcroppings of the mountainside and continued downward, bouncing off the jutting rock face and the lower sections of the winding highway.

The six limousines followed, turning end over end, spilling out their human cargo, which bounced alongside their metal coffins until a shard of rock or a stubborn rock face claimed the pulped remains.

A huge helicopter hovered over a causeway where the four trucks maneuvered to a stop, forming a platform for its landing skids. Assassins scrambled from truck cabs to climb aboard.

To the scores of observers sitting in blocked vehicles, awestruck, the operation looked like a well-rehearsed television stunt. Before anyone could react, the helicopter rose above the crest, cranked up its forward thrust and disappeared across the coastal plane toward Ethiopia.

1

The diner was almost deserted, the early-morning trade thinning out. Bolan had waited until after six before calling Brognola. He had caught a couple of hours sleep in the parking lot of an all-night diner outside Norfolk, and he'd eaten a trencherman breakfast. Brognola was often at his desk by six. Some nights he worked until the small hours and slept on a couch in his office.

"Brognola," the voice of the big grizzled man boomed out.

"I'm just north of Norfolk. Where do you want to meet?" the soldier asked. Both men fully understood the importance of keeping the conversation brief.

"What's your transport?"

"A car. I've got some cargo. Take about four hours. Where?"

"The diner where we met last time. The one with quiet booths in back."

"The one near Howard's?"

"That's the one."

"See you just after ten."

The place was Nate's Diner, just down the street from Howard Johnson's Motor Inn on Virginia Street. It took the warrior just under three hours, with a heavy foot all the way, to make it to Washington. He punished the car up Highway 64 to Richmond, fought his way through the northbound traffic on Interstate 95 to the outskirts of the capital, then needed another hour to make it through city traffic to the diner.

Bolan had done a quick recon of the immediate area, checking out the locale. They had met here before with no problems but you could never be sure. While Bolan hadn't given away his identity or purpose on the phone, he and Brognola had discussed location, vaguely. An unsecure line promoted vagueness.

As he waited for his old friend to arrive, Bolan remembered a rainy afternoon years earlier when Brognola opened up about himself for the first time. The big Fed had talked about the early years of his career, the years of law school, the years he'd been a junior with the Bureau working out of small fleabag offices.

They had talked about the time when the big man from Justice had made much less money but was probably happier. He had talked about choices, something Bolan knew about. Brognola's choice had been to do what he could within the system. Bolan's had been to do what had to be done and stay alive.

They had talked about their unique relationship, something they hadn't done before or since. Only a handful of people knew that Bolan and Brognola helped each other out from time to time. One of them sat behind a desk in the Oval Office.

When the two men had first come up against each other, the Executioner was a hunted fugitive. Yet they had recognized in each other a kindred spirit. Apart from Bolan's very few close associates, Brognola was the only man who truly understood him. It was a deep and abiding friendship that was forged in pain and would only end when one or the other was in the wrong place at the wrong time.

Bolan watched as Brognola parked a half block away and followed his progress to the diner. He waited ten minutes, then walked across the street and went in. The big Fed was seated in a booth at the rear, facing the door. Bolan slid into the seat opposite him.

A waitress sauntered to their table, calling a greeting to a couple of seniors who walked through the door. Bolan and Brognola ordered coffee.

"How'd it go in Norfolk?"

"Deathbed confession," the soldier said. "Case closed."

"That's it, then."

Brognola pulled a cigar from an inner pocket and removed the cellophane wrapper. "Striker, I don't suppose you've seen the papers in the past couple of days. Someone assassinated the king of Saudi Arabia."

Bolan didn't look surprised. "Had to happen some day. The whole family are sitting ducks. How'd it go down?"

"The king and two of his brothers were killed by parties unknown. Pushed their cars off a cliff on a mountain road. The killers were evacuated by helicopter to Ethiopia or Somalia before interceptors could be scrambled."

"And the Saudis are being as tight-lipped as usual?"

"You've got it," Brognola replied, biting off the end of the cigar and shoving the stogie in a corner of his mouth.

"Let's have everything you've got."

"Two of the eight attackers were hit by wild shots from the king's guard. They were killed as they fell from their trucks."

"They used trucks to push them off the road?"

"Yeah, a real sweet job. They used heavy Mercedes transports, the most common truck on the road over there. Ten thousand feet to the bottom. Hell of a way to go."

"You mentioned two of the killers were dead. Any clues?"

"One was an Arab, definitely not a Saudi. The other was a non-Arab. His shoes were eastern European, probably Eastern Bloc. That's all we have. None of our agencies know what happened. If someone knows, he's not talking. The President has asked me to dig into this on the qt. We have to find out who, how and why. Business as usual."

He looked Bolan straight in the eye. "The Saudis don't want any of our people in there officially. Since they found some CIA types operating on phony visas last year, we have no real organization in place. We've managed to get one man in as a flier, a crop duster.

"I need you, Striker," he went on. "If they get someone in the royal family on the throne who favors the East, the whole Gulf area goes. Except for dubious support from the crop duster, you'll be on your own— no real backup. The one man we have will give you an entry into the country. He'll act as a pipeline for funds. You may need a few thousand for grease and expenses."

"Last time I was there, everything cost an arm and a leg."

"It's worse now," the big Fed said. "This job's going to be different in a lot of ways. You might have to call on me for help. You know the frequencies to use. The Corps of Engineers will be the conduit."

"What's the real motive?" Bolan asked. "I know that wealth might be a factor, but do we have anything else? Anything political like the Soviets?"

"My people don't know yet and they may never find out," Brognola admitted. "The fact is, we can't afford to have Saudi continuity disturbed.

"The Saudis are the key to Gulf oil," he continued. "We're counting on them to cooperate with our convoying Kuwait shipping out of the Gulf."

"That's it?" Bolan asked.

"No. The CIA chief of station in London has assigned a Middle East expert to help. The COS won't get involved personally, but he might line up a better cover."

AT HEATHROW taxis lined up to carry fares beyond the local area. A burly cockney opened the front door next to where Bolan stood, waited until the warrior tossed in his bag and then asked, "Where to, mate?"

"Sloane Square."

"Just in from the States, are you?" the cabbie asked as he maneuvered through the labyrinth of roads leading out of the airport proper.

"Yeah." Bolan wasn't inclined toward small talk and focused his attention on the passing scenery. He didn't know why his contact had insisted they meet at a hotel in Belgravia, but he assumed it was a place where they could talk undisturbed.

The cabbie got the message. He kept his eyes on the road and his mouth shut as they moved slowly down the M4, crowded by trucks and buses heading for riverside terminals at midafternoon. They were well into the heart of Kensington before he asked, "You want the hotel at Sloane Square, mate?"

"Yeah. The Royal Court."

In minutes Bolan was dropped off. He entered the bar, as arranged, and spotted his man, a tall slim guy wearing tweeds who didn't look much different from other men in the bar, which was reserved for registered guests.

"Brad Masters." The CIA man held out a slim hand.

Bolan shook the hand and nodded curtly. He was in no mood for preliminaries. "What have you set up?" he asked.

"You have to go in alone, fly into the Sudan, Civil Airport, Khartoum. You take delivery of a Cessna 172 and fly it in under their radar. You have an American passport in the name of Mike Ford." The slim man spoke in short, clipped phrases, a passable imitation of his MI-6 counterparts. He'd probably been on the London assignment too long. He paused to take a sip of his pint, looking at Bolan over the rim of his glass. "You will work with Christy Connors. He runs a two-man pesticide air service for the minister of agriculture. He's a naturalized American. We haven't had him long, and I wouldn't count on him for much."

Bolan didn't bother to answer. Instead, he asked, "You set up a flight to Khartoum?"

"Eight tomorrow morning."

"Tomorrow?"

"I don't want to rush you in too fast. Saudi Arabia isn't like most countries. You've got to have a reason for being in the country or you get shipped out in a hurry. The police—the CID internal security people—will keep a close watch on someone like you."

"I've had it happen before," Bolan said dryly, amused by his own understatement.

"I've given you the best cover we have, but I'm trying to do better," Masters went on. "The ones who planned the killing aren't going anywhere. We believe they'll kill again."

"What do you mean, 'better'?"

"An agent of ours in Khartoum may be available. A Sudanese. He can fly you in, do what he can to help. If we can't set you up with our man, you can fly, can't you?"

"I can manage. Am I booked in here?"

"Yes. Why don't you get a few hours of sleep? I'll send a car for you at six." Masters signed his chit and rose to leave.

Bolan sat for a moment and thought about the job ahead.

The Saudis had been conned by every race and creed since oil money had made them a target, and they had grown to suspect everything and everyone. He couldn't blame them. But they went too far. He would be more shut off from help there than if he'd been behind the iron curtain. And the police would be on him like a blanket if they even suspected he was anything other than what he appeared to be.

THE BRITISH AIRWAYS FLIGHT to Khartoum took off at eight as scheduled. Bolan ordered a brandy and relaxed.

The flight progressed uneventfully until several hours later the Sudan came at them out of the vastness of the upper Nile. Khartoum appeared as a green oasis surrounded by the hovels of the poor. The airport had been a beauty spot of its own at one time, but was now ringed by the hastily erected concrete block houses of the middle class and the cardboard shacks of the less fortunate.

As the plane circled, Bolan could see a group of private aircraft on the south tarmac, and assumed his Cessna would be one of these.

The check through customs and immigration was time-consuming, as the mad overtures of Colonel Khaddafi in the northwest were making these people very cautious.

As the warrior finally cleared immigration, a Sudanese approached him. He was dressed in the manner of the hillmen of the Upper Nile. His head was swathed in a white turban twisted in multifolds around his head, its two-foot long tail hanging down his back. He wore a *gabalia* from chin to toe similar to the Saudi *thobe* but fuller, flared more at the bottom.

"I am Zaki Abdul Rachman Jabbar," the man said, grabbing Bolan's hand and pumping it enthusiastically. "I will fly the Cessna." He grinned as he released the powerful hand, obviously pleased to be included in the mission.

"Mike Ford."

Jabbar's dark skin had an almost bluish hue. His perfect teeth shone like beacons in a face that seemed to be one perpetual smile. He was almost as tall as Bolan, a black-and-white being who radiated warmth and friendship. The warrior hoped the man possessed a certain degree of toughness beneath his easy manner.

The Sudanese had a jeep close to the entrance to the small terminal. They drove around to the civilian field. Their brand-new aircraft stood apart from the others. Any 172 Bolan had ever flown always had the stamp of someone else's heavy hand upon it. This one had been assembled in Europe and equipped for the CIA. The radio was a King KX170B with 720 channels and had an effective range of a thousand miles, depending on altitude.

Connors's camp was about three hundred miles from Dhahran, so he knew he could relay messages from the Corps of Engineers to Brognola from there. If the enemy camp was more than five hundred miles from Dhahran, he might be out of range. The small plane had extended-range fuel tanks, an automatic pilot and a lot of other electronic gadgets. If Bolan managed to get in and out as fast as he hoped, most of the gadgets would never be used.

Jabbar wasted no time. He was required to file a flight plan, so he filed one for Jidda and took off in a hurry. The Sudanese took the Cessna directly over Berber and onward to the Nubian Desert.

"Your weapons came in by diplomatic courier," the Sudanese said as soon as he could relax. He hesitated. "Let us dispense with formalities. I will call you Mike, and you will call me Zaki. The briefcase is in the back, Mike."

"Thanks. Masters used our consulate?"

"No. He works closely with MI-6. They pass more than we do through their conduit. No one seems to suspect the British. Not like they mistrust Americans.

"Do you wish to take over?" Jabbar continued. "She handles quite well."

Bolan hadn't handled the controls of a small aircraft for some time. Maybe it would be a good idea to get his hand in. He stayed in the right seat and reached for the control bar.

"Masters told me you speak Arabic," Jabbar said.

"He was wrong. I understand a lot if it's spoken slowly—catch a few words when someone talks fast."

"Then I will interpret."

They had reached the Red Sea, which was about a hundred and fifty miles across at this point. Bolan flew up the middle of the body of water to a point well north of the Saudi city of Medina, then turned east, making land just south of Dhaba.

To this point, he had been maintaining an altitude of just over a hundred feet. Fingers of radar scanned their territory, and the Saudi AWACS planes were up. A hundred miles inland he had to climb to six thousand feet to cross the Uwayrid Mountains. He had the radio on international intercept frequency but didn't hear a single call. As he reached the southern edge of An-Nafud, the Red Desert, he was back to a hundred feet and unchallenged.

Suddenly the radio crackled. "This is Saudi Air Force AWACS 100. Identify. Small aircraft over the Nafud, identify."

This was just what he'd feared. If he couldn't pull it off, they'd scramble a couple of F-16s from the base at Hail.

He pushed the talk button. "Cessna SA540 registered to Farsi and Connors Pesticide. You have us on your list. Over."

He waited tensely while they checked. "Confirmed. You are on the list. Please state the number of your ministerial edict."

Bolan had to pull a duplicate set of papers from his bag. He juggled the control bar, the microphone and the papers as the ship yawed left and right at low altitude.

Jabbar grabbed for the bar on his side.

"Hold it a minute." Bolan put the microphone down while he searched, glad that Masters had insisted he had a copy of their authorization. "Here it is," he said. "Edict number SAM17776."

"Got to check the computer. Hold your current heading."

The line went dead for a full minute, then squawked to life. "Roger. That verifies. Hey—where did you pop up from?" The Texas drawl took on a less formal tone. "We only had you on scope for a minute or two back there."

"Flew out of Tabuk on my way back to our camp at Majma'a," Bolan said, taking control of the ship again, trying to sound casual. "I have to hedgehop to inspect foliage for infestation. You probably picked me up in the mountains."

"Man, you sound like a good old boy. Over."

"As American as mom's apple pie," the soldier answered, trying to sound like the Texan. "What are you guys doing calling yourselves the Saudi air force?"

"Haven't been able to train these yahoos yet. Got to fly the patterns ourselves."

Bolan wondered if their base monitored all their transmissions. They were probably recorded while airborne and evaluated later by review boards.

"So what else is new?" he asked. "Do I have your blessing to go home for a beer?"

"If you got beer, old buddy, we might get this crate down at your place."

"Great to be among friends. You sound as relaxed as hell," Bolan said.

"You bet. It gets awful lonely in this here sky, pardner," the cowpoke voice came back. "Don't speak to anyone for hours."

"Cut the gab, Lieutenant." The pilot had finally had enough sense to shut his man down. "This isn't the barracks block."

"Yes, sir."

The speaker squawked in his ear again. "You take care now, you hear? Over."

A slight smile raised Bolan's lips. The kid would never learn. He pushed his talk button for the last time. "Roger and out."

Maybe the real danger was past. He didn't think that other ground radar could get a fix on him. He scanned the horizon, picked up the western edge of the thin line that marked another desert, Ad-Dahna, and followed it south. Masters's map showed Connors's camp at the edge of the desert about ten miles north of a town called Majma'a.

JABBAR SAT QUIETLY while Bolan flew the plane. Once in a while he glanced at his new colleague, sizing him up. He had the feeling of being in the presence of raw power. A sense of danger seemed to emanate from the man. He would be a bad one to cross.

Masters had used Jabbar as a runner, picking up messages at drops in East Africa. Occasionally they would meet secretly in Cairo where the COS would use him as a courier or pass on instructions for jobs in the Sudan, Ethiopia or Somalia. As a pilot, Jabbar was sought after by the intelligence community. He'd chosen the CIA because the pay was better. Loyalty or beliefs had played no part in his decision.

Everyone knew everyone else in the so-called covert game that was played in the Middle East and Africa. It was probably the same for agents all over the world, a game for boys who hadn't grown into men, hide-and-seek or cloak-and-dagger with real daggers and real bullets.

It had been different for him lately. He had committed the ultimate sin for an agent—he had a loving wife and he was a father. But it was too late for recriminations. He had a son, and fatherhood had changed him. He was still the same man who had served in his country's army and been sent to the United States for flight training, but he worried more about coming home from a mission. He rarely pulled his gun and only when severely provoked. He took fewer chances.

The Sudanese looked out the window at the Arabian countryside passing beneath him. He loved flying. It always gave him a sense of peace. This time, with his man, that feeling wouldn't come. It wasn't that the man evoked a spirit of evil; rather he created an aura of conflict that could only be resolved by a final and conclusive act. He couldn't see compromise in this stranger; couldn't see pity. What he could see was a certain ruthlessness and unwavering dedication. It made him feel uncomfortable.

He shifted in his seat and felt the weight of his gun under his robe. It had never bothered him before. He'd seldom fired it, but he had a feeling that would change.

ALL THE TOWNS looked the same to Bolan. There were scores of them, hundreds of concrete block structures, a few water towers and thousands of goats. He moved west and followed the highway out of Buraida, a town described to him as having the largest marketplace in the Nejd, the central plateau. They flew southeast of Zilfi. Jabbar pointed out the jail, the only one in the area. They continued on to Majma'a where the king and his brother, the crown prince, had built twin palaces. The gleaming structures on the southern outskirts were the town landmarks.

Bolan turned east from the town and circled to the north. The land was flat semidesert, dotted with groupings of buttes, flat-topped outcroppings rising to three or four hundred feet. The area reminded him of Arizona and New Mexico, but he knew it was much hotter.

"You see any sign of a camp?" he asked Jabbar over the sounds of the engine.

"Can't see anything special, Mike," the Sudanese replied. "Lots of tracks in the hardpan but no sign of a camp."

Bolan searched in ever-widening circles for a half hour. His fuel gauge showed he was half-empty. He saw no sign of civilization.

Suddenly he saw it. In an area between four towering buttes, a second Cessna sat close to three small tents.

Something was wrong.

He throttled back, letting the plane take him closer at minimum speed. A body lay near one of the tents, a land vehicle sat deserted on the hardpan—the camp had been ransacked.

Bolan made several passes to confirm what he'd seen. He scouted the area and came up with a similar clustering of buttes three miles closer to Ad-Dahna. Bringing the Cessna down carefully, he landed close to the buttes and taxied between them, away from curious eyes, then turned the plane around to face the opening he had entered.

Before he removed his personal weapons from the briefcase, Bolan opened both doors for ventilation. They'd been on the ground for less than five minutes, and the inside of the plane was like an oven.

Armed with his Beretta 93-R, Bolan, accompanied by Jabbar, slipped to the desert floor and started the three-mile hike to the camp. As he walked from the cover of the buttes into the sun, he wondered if he'd made a mistake. Three miles through the heat of Arabia in the open was like five miles in Death Valley. But he wanted the Cessna in a safe place, and he wanted to approach the camp cautiously. The deserted camp was a question mark.

Keeping small rock formations and scrub between themselves and the camp, they took more than an hour to cover the three miles. Bolan was close to dehydration, and his shirt was soaked. The soles of his feet were baked, despite sturdy hiking boots.

The damage to the camp was much worse when viewed close up. Connors had been shot by an automatic weapon, the slugs stitching him from groin to temple, blowing away half of his head. He lay on his back. Pools of blood, almost black, had soaked into the hardpan. Three huge vultures were perched on his stomach and shoulders, pulling at the shredded flesh of his chest.

Jabbar turned away and retched.

Bolan picked up a coil of rope and swung it over his head, chasing the birds. They flew twenty feet away and sat, waiting.

The warrior inspected the camp. It seemed that nothing of value had been taken, though almost everything had been trashed and scattered to the wind. He found Connors's authorization papers from the ministry on the passenger seat of the camp's Cessna. He folded them into a pocket of his safari shirt. The vehicle near the airplane was a fairly new four-wheel-drive Suburban, which was equipped for desert travel.

Bolan knew he could accomplish nothing here. Connors had been his only contact, and he was dead. There were no footprints in the hardpan, but the Executioner did find several shell casings from the automatic weapon used in the killing. They told him little. They might be Soviet-made, but he couldn't be sure. They weren't from a Soviet AK or any American automatic weapon. He sat for a few minutes at the camp table, took a can of orange juice from the nearby cooler and waited for his strength to return. The cooler still had ice. Conners had been dead for less than twenty-four hours. One thing was clear—he no longer had a conduit to money or supplies.

Bolan rolled heavy cans of pesticide to form a shelter around the body and packed the Suburban with two cases of bottled water and a box of canned goods. When Jabbar recovered, they drove off, heading across the desert to their own Cessna. It was time to report in.

The heat, an oven even in the Suburban, took a lot out of Bolan. When they got to the plane, he climbed into it, paused to drink some water, flicked a switch and waited for a moment to compose himself. The KX170B crackled to life, bringing in the Corps of Engineers channel at Dhahran with no trouble. Bolan sent out his report to Justice. Within minutes a message would be relayed to the U.S. and Brognola would know that Connors was dead, and that Bolan was out in the cold. If the big Fed wanted to send instructions, he would respond.

After twenty minutes of baking in the blistering heat, Bolan heard a familiar voice over the radio. It was Brognola. "Where are you, Striker?"

"Near Connors's camp. There's nothing more I can do. I have the original edict from the minister. It might be useful later. Anything new from your end?"

"Two more brothers dead. The Saudis are paranoid. Don't attract attention to yourself." Brognola knew the Executioner didn't have to be told, but on rare occasions his feelings showed.

"I'm going to leave this plane hidden," Bolan said. "It's in a fairly central location, depending where the enemy is holed up. I'll use the radio report if necessary."

"Will you need help getting out?"

Bolan knew the big man was anxious. "I don't plan on getting out just yet. I plan to use the Cessna eventually, unless that becomes impossible. What about the AWACS planes? Seems they're manned by our people."

"We can't use those guys. You've got to stay clear. They have the most sophisticated electronic scanning equipment we can devise on board, and the Saudis have paid us good money for it. Best to avoid them."

"Roger. I've got a man, a Sudanese my contact in London set up. He's a pilot. Could be a lot of help."

"Don't play around on this one, Striker. Kill the whole thing dead at all costs, and do it fast. Find out who's masterminding the killing and terminate him. No hint of American involvement. Understood?"

"I heard you the first time, pal," Bolan said over the fast-fading line.

"My orders are to keep it low-key," Brognola reminded him.

"Nothing unusual about that. Will you be in town long?"

"I don't plan on going anywhere."

"I'll probably need some money. Better scare up some Saudi currency. I'll call on this frequency."

"Good enough. Take care, Striker."

Bolan signed off and slipped down from the cabin of the plane.

2

Bolan followed his own tracks back to the pesticide camp and knew it was a mistake as he neared Connors's Cessna. A black GMC Jimmy stood next to the plane, and two men holding machine pistols waited for the Suburban to come to a stop.

Bolan was tempted to make a run for it but knew they could radio ahead. Better to find out what the hell was going on then to become a fugitive in his first hour on Saudi soil.

"Do you have a gun?" he asked Jabbar.

"Yes."

"Keep it out of sight. If they speak English, let me do the talking."

He pulled up near the Jimmy and slipped from the driver's seat cautiously, keeping twenty feet between him and the intruders.

"Why is your plane not here with the other?" one of the men asked in Oxford English.

"Who are you?" Bolan asked, ignoring the question.

"Central Intelligence Department, Saudi national guard," one of the men replied. "You will raise your arms and answer the question."

Bolan raised his arms casually. "What's happened to my partner?"

"My question," the second man said. "We will find out at our headquarters."

"We don't know anything about this," Bolan protested. "We just flew in."

"So you say," the first man said, moving forward to search him for weapons. "But we have a chief who assumes you are guilty until proved otherwise."

A gun barked suddenly, and one of the men went down, blood from a head wound splattering his companion.

As Bolan turned, his eyes took in the scene like an action shot from a high-speed camera. Jabbar was standing close by, holding a gun in a two-handed grip. One of the CID men was slumping to the ground. The other was bringing his gun to bear on the Sudanese.

Bolan whipped the Beretta from its holster and had it trained on the other man before he could fire. "Drop it," he commanded.

The Saudi ignored him. Bolan went with the man's play, knocking the gun to the sand with his free hand as he clubbed him with his own weapon.

He turned on the Sudanese. "What was that all about? You can't kill everyone who pulls out a gun. These men were only doing their job."

Jabbar was stunned by his own actions. He shook himself and slipped his weapon back into the folds of his robe. "You asked me if I had a gun. I thought—"

"Never mind. It's already hit the fan. Let's get out of here."

Jabbar pulled a coil of rope from the bed of the Suburban, moved some of the pesticide cans and started to slip the rope around the dead men.

"What are you doing?"

"We can't leave the bodies here for the vultures to signal their position," he said as he started to drag the corpses of Connors and the CID man to the tailgate of the truck. He tied them heels first so that their shoulders would drag in the dust. The bodies were in line with the tire tracks. Jabbar prepared to tow them away while Bolan examined the unconscious man, who had a lump the size of an egg on his temple. He'd be out for a while. Bolan dragged him to the shade of some pesticide cans, left a bottle of water beside him and headed for the Suburban.

"If we pull up some bushes and tie them to the police Jimmy, maybe we can cover the tracks to the Cessna what the bodies might miss," Jabbar suggested.

Bolan wasn't happy with the whole deal, but he didn't argue. He might be carrying out the mission, but this was his companion's world. They pulled several dried-out thornbushes from the desert floor and tied them to the rear of the Jimmy.

Jabbar drove the Suburban, the bodies stirring up a cloud of dust behind. He followed the faint tire tracks partway to the Cessna, then peeled off to the west.

Bolan followed, driving the Jimmy and towing the bushes in the Suburban's wake. A couple of miles into the desert he got out to see the effect of his work. His tracks were totally cleared. The almost daily dust storms would do the rest. He passed the point where Jabbar had turned off, dragged the bushes almost to the Cessna, then veered off to join the Suburban a few miles to the west where Jabbar was untying his load.

The vultures had followed. Before Bolan had abandoned the Jimmy and joined Jabbar in the other vehicle, the birds were at work tearing at the remains of Connors and the dead cop. Bolan looked on quietly for a few seconds. It wasn't the birds that bothered him. Nature had her own way of doing things. It was the dead cop.

It was exactly fifteen miles from the four buttes to the highway south of Majma'a. Bolan told Jabbar to stop while they took a bearing. He could see the buttes near the pesticide camp in the distance and beyond to the distinctive three-fingered butte where his Cessna waited. He found a derelict oil drum, stood it erect on the side of the road and piled four small rocks on top in the shape of a pyramid. Bedouin frequently left such signs to mark their camps. The sign wouldn't be disturbed by anyone. Bolan got back into the Suburban and saw that Jabbar had fallen asleep in the back seat. He shook his head, got behind the steering wheel and started the engine.

A black ribbon of new asphalt stretched out to the south as far as the Executioner could see. He pushed the Suburban up to seventy-five and held it there, keeping an eye on the odometer. After ten miles he came to Al-Auda, another guidepost to remember. Now he could relax. The heat built up, and a smell of melting asphalt entered the air intake. He turned on the front air conditioner.

Traffic increased as they approached Riyadh. Every hundred yards or so a wrecked car or a dead camel lay in studied silence, reminding him of the danger of Saudi highway travel. Halfway to Riyadh he saw two gasoline tankers welded together, smoking hulks of cooling metal, the last abode of two impatient drivers.

As Bolan approached Riyadh from the north an hour later, the new airport was a surprise to him. It was immense. He saw a new national guard housing development next to the airport followed by the sprawling

University of Riyadh. All the development reminded him of the background information he'd read on the flight to Heathrow. It had covered the way the Saudis spent their oil money. They must be into—what had Brognola's intelligence said?—their third five-year plan? The money had to be flowing like water.

He continued through the outskirts of the city, past the old airport where three converted Boeing 707s, sporting huge mushroom-shaped domes over their fuselages, were parked. This was obviously the AWACS base. He continued south on Airport Road.

The road changed to King Faisal Street closer to the downtown area. As the central crossover, a spaghetti junction of turnoffs, he turned east to Batha Street and the El-Khureigi Hotel. It had been the most modern hotel in the city on his first visit to Riyadh years ago but now well down the list, a refuge for the lower fringe of international salesmen.

Bolan parked the Suburban out back next to the bus terminal.

"I'll register here. We'd better stay in different hotels," he told Jabbar. "You know one that's close by?"

"I have friends near here," the Sudanese said, rubbing sleep from his eyes.

"I'll meet you in the lobby in one hour."

Bolan registered as Mike Ford. The lobby, not as elegant as he remembered, was crowded. It smelled of hard work and old men. When the police registration had been completed, he held out his hand for his passport.

"I'm sorry, Mr. Ford," the clerk apologized. "Since the trouble, we are ordered to retain passports until departure." The clerk, an Egyptian, spoke in English, which was the second language of Saudi Arabia.

"No problem." Bolan took the key and found his way to the fifth floor. The room was plain, but it was reasonably clean, smelling of soap and polish. He opened the curtains and looked out, taking in the spectacular view of the city.

It was almost dark, but he couldn't resist one tour around town before he packed it in for the day. Perhaps he and Jabbar could make a tour of the souks and have dinner at a local restaurant. As an American he might learn little, but there was always tomorrow and there was always Jabbar.

First, he had to cover himself. If the Saudis were making any security sweeps during the emergency, his weapons and papers couldn't be explained away. He wrapped the Beretta and his combat knife in a towel. In a smaller towel he hid his European funds and the papers he'd taken from Connors. He kept a copy of Connors's authorization papers in an inside pocket with the rest of his money.

Bolan opened the door and looked out. All was quiet. He moved across the hall and picked the lock to the linen closet, where shelves were piled high with bed sheets and towels. He shoved his package in at the bottom and straightened the pile.

Jabbar was waiting in the lobby. They got into the Suburban and headed away from the bus terminal, with its hundreds of idle buses, all painted garishly by their owners. He turned toward Batha Street and south to the old town. It was the worst time of day to drive—if any time was safe in Riyadh. The Saudis believed whatever happened was the will of God, and they drove as if possessed of His immunity.

Bolan waited for a red light. Several cars filled with Saudi youths barreled through in front of him. As the light turned green and he started through, a Mercedes came out of nowhere, broadsiding the Suburban behind the driver's door.

The tortured screech of metal was the only thing Bolan remembered clearly. He was flung toward the point of impact, his head hitting the padded passenger door.

THE EGYPTIAN NURSE was fat. She stood beside a bed in a private room fussing with a thermometer, trying to get it down to normal before she shoved it into her patient's mouth.

The door opened and a tall, handsome officer entered. "Leave us," he ordered in Arabic. His voice was quiet but authoritative.

She swiveled her massive hips to leave, her eyes meeting his briefly. Then she turned and increased her pace, putting distance between herself and the man she both knew and feared.

"Can you hear me, Ahmed?" the man said. He removed his headdress and dropped it into the chair beside him. The crossed swords and palms of the national guard insignia was clipped to the cloth. It clattered on to the chipped paint of the chair.

"Captain. Yes," the wounded man replied. "I'm not as bad as they probably told you. A headache. Maybe a little dehydrated."

"Tell me about the ones who did this to you."

"A tall black man shot Fawzi. He was dressed in Sudanese robes and turban. The other was a big man, not fat but taller than his companion, and muscular," the officer said, holding a hand to his head. "He had piercing eyes, hard eyes. Light, I think."

"He was a foreigner?"

"American. He didn't seem to know about the death of Connors. He'd come to be a partner. That's what he said."

"He was the man who clubbed you?"

"He carried a gun. He could have shot me when I was watching Fawzi going down. But he didn't. He clubbed me instead."

"Don't worry, Ahmed," the captain said, his face grim. "We'll get the foreign devil. And when we do, he will not be shot as your partner was shot. We'll let the courts and the sword deal with him."

BOLAN OPENED HIS EYES and groaned as pain filled his head. Jabbar was beside him, either asleep or unconscious, a lump on his head, his turban a pile of blood-stained loose cloth in his lap.

The soldier looked around. They were in a cell with forty or fifty other men, the dregs of the streets. Every man sat on the concrete floor or tried to curl up next to the bars.

Bolan's head throbbed. He ran his hand over his forehead, touching a two-inch gash that accounted for the dried blood that covered most of his forehead and crusted in his eyebrows.

The damned Mercedes. He had barely seen it in his peripheral vision before the crash.

He looked at Jabbar. The Sudanese was breathing regularly. When Bolan turned him over and shook one shoulder, Jabbar opened his eyes and grinned.

"Allah is good. We are still alive, Mike," he said, his voice surprisingly clear and calm.

"Where are we?"

"I was only partly conscious when they brought us in, but I'm sure this is the central jail."

"Next to the courts and the clock tower?" Bolan asked.

"The infamous tower." He pointed to two men leaning against the bars, their eyes haunted by some unknown fear. "I heard someone say those two would be executed in the morning."

"Nothing's changed. Friday morning executions at the foot of the clock tower."

"Be thankful it is not us," the small man said. "If they connect us to the dead policeman in the desert, we will be on next Friday's list."

Bolan knew Jabbar was right. He felt in his pockets for the papers he carried and found nothing. It had been stupid not to hide them with his other papers. They tied him to Connors like an umbilical.

Had the CID men radioed back before their encounter? Had they found the man Bolan had knocked unconscious? Did their superiors know about Connors's death? It didn't matter. The fact that they had been sent to investigate the camp and were missing was enough.

He knew the routine. A quick trial before the ulema, a group of religious men, the interpreters of the Koran, the word of Mohammed that served as their civil law. Then a sharp blade swung by powerful hands to the base of an unprotected neck the next holy day, a Friday, one week from tomorrow.

No way. They would have to get out, and soon.

As the thoughts played out possibilities in his tired brain, two guards marched down the corridor outside the cell. One opened the door while the other stood back, the M-16 in his hands cocked and ready.

The guard with the keys barked a command.

"They want us to follow," Jabbar said.

Bolan followed Jabbar through the door and down the corridor between the two guards. They had his authorization papers for the pesticide operation. No point in lying. He'd stick close to the truth—close enough, but not too close. He was Mike Ford. He had been to the camp and found it vandalized. He whispered the scenario to Jabbar.

"We were coming in to report the ruined camp at the time of the accident. We never saw a body or the CID men—"

"Hallas!" one of the guards shouted. "Enough."

"Don't worry, Mike," Jabbar said from a corner of his mouth. "I know the score. We never saw Connors or anyone. Our papers disappeared at the accident scene. Thieves, right?"

"Right."

"Hallas!" the guard shouted again as they came to a massive oak door at the end of a long hallway two floors above the cells.

They were pushed in by the guards, the M-16 barrels bruising their backs.

A uniformed man sat at a massive desk on a dais. The office was large, ringed with black leather sofa chairs in the Saudi fashion. Petitioners and hangers-on sat in most of them, drinking sweet tea from clear glass mugs and watching, amused expressions on their hawklike faces.

The man in charge wore the uniform of a captain— the national guard Bolan guessed—probably CID. His face was grim beneath the red-checked *guttra*. A metal badge was clipped to the cloth at his forehead, an insignia, crossed swords with palms. The Saudi's features were rock-hard, not unlike Bolan's, strong and intimidating. He was a big man, muscular and fit.

"I am Captain Ibrahim Sedik," the officer announced in cultured English. "It was my man you killed yesterday."

The words had been spit out. No preliminaries. No explanations. Bolan decided to say nothing. At this point he had nothing to lose by keeping his mouth shut.

"We found one of my men still alive. Kill one but not the other. Strange," he mused. "We also found their vehicle and the bones the vultures had left," Sedik continued grimly. "I want the whole story. Who are you, Mr. Ford, citizen of the United States? I have Connors's papers. They name you as a partner. You were carrying nothing else."

Bolan decided to give him something. "We were coming in to report the vandalism and the death of Connors," he said, wiping a hand across his blood-encrusted forehead. "We know nothing of your men. The accident . . . I don't remember . . ."

"Yes, the accident. The sons of two of our prominent citizens were killed in the accident, Mr. Ford. We'll have to add that to your crimes."

"I flew in here legally. The camp was vandalized and the sons of your friends drove into me. What's going on here, Captain? You looking for a goat?"

"Oh no you don't. That doesn't work here, Mr. Ford," the policeman said, a sneer in his voice. "Here we look at facts, listen to the lies of the accused, then judge for ourselves. The ulema will want revenge for the deaths of good Saudis."

Bolan started to protest, but knew it was useless. The Saudi system was as filled with holes on the side of swift justice as the American system was on the side of merciful and prolonged trials and appeals. His fate was sealed. He had to find another way.

"Take them away," the captain ordered. "They will see the ulema in two days."

3

On the way back to the cells, Bolan studied the layout of the building. The upper floors weren't well guarded. The toughest part would be getting out of the basement cells, and negotiating the long stairway to the first level.

Now was not the time. The guards were too alert. They kept their M-16s trained on the prisoners, allowing no opportunity to take them out. The Executioner decided to give it a little time. His head still throbbed. The pain nauseated him, and with the nausea came a weakness that made him less than his best. Maybe tomorrow would be better. They would know more about the jail, and he'd probably be feeling stronger.

At the lower level one guard opened the cell and stood back. The only empty space was next to an Eastern-style toilet. Bolan stood in the middle of the room and studied the men around him.

They grinned at him through blackened and broken teeth, Pakistanis, Saudis, Yemenis and a mixture of other Middle Easterners, all filthy, dressed in rags. He was the foreigner, the infidel, the outsider.

A huge Pakistani hill man sat beside the cell door, looking up at Bolan. He had won the best place in the cell by brute strength and wasn't about to give it up.

Bolan stood in front of the Pakistani, and the man saw no fear in the warrior's eyes, only confidence. The Executioner feinted with a booted left foot, and when the Pakistani tried for it, clubbed him on the side of the head with clenched fists.

The hill man slumped against the bars, and Bolan dragged the inert body into the center of the room, glaring coldly at the men who sat next to the space vacated by the Pakistani. They moved grudgingly to make room for Bolan and Jabbar.

As Bolan settled himself as comfortably as the concrete floor would permit, the big Pakistani shook his ragged head of dead man's hair, a mop that had never seen a comb. He pulled himself to his knees, growled deep in his throat like a wild animal, and came at Bolan, his arms outstretched.

The Executioner and his Sudanese companion were trapped, sitting with their backs against the bars. The whole cell was quiet as breaths were drawn in.

Bolan waited until the huge man had committed himself and was almost upon them. He bent one knee and levered the sole and heel of his booted foot into the charging man, catching him in the crotch.

The Pakistani collapsed against them, his weight taking them sideways to the floor. Bolan squirmed out from under the big man and pushed him toward the middle of the room.

The fight was over almost before it had even begun.

After a few minutes, the guards wandered down the corridor and the cell settled down for the night. Bolan told Jabbar to keep his eyes open and curled up for a few minutes of sleep.

CAPTAIN SEDIK SAT at his massive desk on the dais, looking down on his best men, all in native dress, their military garb discarded to give them anonymity on the street.

Sedik still wore the uniform of a captain of the national guard, the pride of the CID. He was aware that his uniform and the headdress, combined with strong and intimidating features, served him best in situations like this. The dais and the furniture added to the appearance of strength and invulnerability.

Much of the time Sedik didn't feel either strong or invulnerable. He had fought his way to the top, using every tactic at his command. A Bedouin whose family had come from Baha in the mountains, his father hadn't been graced by the patronage of the district governor. The senior Sedik hadn't imitated the fawning attention of his peers, hadn't spent long hours flattering local officialdom and therefore hadn't been favored with contracts or grants that were making his neighbors rich during the rise of oil revenues. When the money trickled down from government to princes to emirs to the people, he hadn't been standing in line, groveling for favors. His pride had given the younger Sedik, the fourth and youngest son, a handicap it would take him twenty years to overcome.

He had joined the national guard. He had been cuffed around and reviled as a recruit. A determined teenager, he had taken what they had to dish out and prospered as much as was possible in the service. In early postings he had learned the art of culling baksheesh from local merchants. As he rose from private to noncom and eventually to second lieutenant, the baksheesh grew. The trick was not to be too greedy and to pass a reasonable share up the line. The lessons were well learned.

As Sedik matured, he knew his life would be spent in the service. The national guard was far better than the fighting services. As a member of the local police, he was closer to the people and benefited from their largess, while army and air force types were confined to military bases and lived on military pay.

He was careful to develop contacts who were privileged to sup at the trough that fed the richest men in Saudi. At an early age he saw the real opportunity, as the chief of the Criminal Investigation Division, and worked toward the post with a vengeance. He had used flattery, guile and performance to claw his way upward. Only once had he used violence to get where he was. His most serious rival had suffered a car accident while vacationing in Cannes. An errant truck had pushed his car off a cliff. Sedik had mourned his passing while paying off the assassin who had carried out the hit.

Today he was at the top of his profession and wouldn't have accepted a higher office if one was offered. All major payoffs to the police came through him. He dutifully passed the money up the line, after taking his cut. Actually he took two pieces of the pie, the part that was his due, and another share, much larger, that was a product of a skimming mechanism he'd learned from experts outside the kingdom.

Sedik was a complex man. He squirreled away his ill-gotten wealth in foreign real estate. And though he maintained a modest demeanor within the kingdom, he lived like a king when abroad. Yet all the while he was the best chief of CID the Saudi national guard had ever had. His record was exceptional. The one blot, which was shared by the military, was the royal deaths that were occurring right under his nose. He would go to any lengths to find the killer, or killers, and put them out of their misery.

He looked down on his best men and started the session. "I know we have the American in a cell and we'll let the ulema pass sentence on him, but I want to know everything possible about the man and I want it in the next thirty-six hours." Sedik's face was a mask of granite. "I want an airtight case. When the Americans write their letters of censure to our foreign minister, I want a story that will paint Ford as black as his own heart. Is that clear enough?"

The half-dozen men nodded solemnly.

"This man probably killed his partner, and we're sure he killed one of our own. *One of our own!*" he repeated, pounding on the massive desk.

"Is he suspected in the deaths?" one of the men asked. He didn't have to explain he meant the deaths within the royal family. They were all tuned in to the deaths so closely that they related everything to it.

"Wouldn't that be convenient?" Sedik mused. "Try to find out if he is. Try to make it look like he is. Our religious brothers will have his head in a few days, so all of you get busy. I want proof that this man is the worst kind of criminal. I want him tied to the royal deaths."

"Will he be questioned, as well?" a hulking man in a dark gray robe asked.

"I plan to let him rot in a cell first, take some of the confidence out of him," the captain replied. "Then we'll question him just before the ulema see him."

When the others had gone, the captain's chief lieutenant stood beside his chair. "Do you think the American suspects your sidelines?" he asked.

"Probably. That's why I want him out of the way fast. It doesn't really matter if he knows about us," the captain said. "He'll be dead in a few days. Who's he going to tell?"

"Do you really think he's the one we seek?" the lieutenant pressed.

"Does he fit the pattern? Can you see him commanding the rabble that pushed the king off the road?"

"No. He's got something else going," the junior officer said.

"Then don't bother me with stupid questions," Sedik growled, turning away from his man and picking up the phone. "We both know he's not the one we want. But he'll do very nicely until someone better shows up."

THE NIGHT PASSED with the Sudanese talking away to anyone who would listen. Bolan rested quietly, trying to formulate some kind of plan for a breakout.

Just before dawn, the two condemned men, as if on cue, started to moan. They knew they were going to die in another hour. Bolan had seen death make its appearance in too many ways to be as affected as the others, but he sympathized with these two. To know you were going to be dragged out to face the swordsman in an hour had to be the ultimate horror. In more civilized countries they drugged the condemned long before the event.

In the hour before they came for the men, Jabbar told Bolan everything he'd learned about the layout of the building and what was going to happen outside.

"The captain accepts bribes from everyone. The law means nothing to him."

"What about killing one of his men?"

"That one doesn't care. He had two faces. He pretends to care, but money is his master."

"Are you sure? These people will see him as they want. He might be straight," Bolan said.

"You can judge for yourself when you see him in action," the Sudanese told him. "They tell me he questions prisoners himself before they see the religious priests for judgment."

"Sounds like we don't want to be around for him to play with. What about this place?" the Executioner asked. "What did you find out?"

"The best time might be right at the time of executions," Jabbar suggested. "Everyone will be distracted."

"How will we know the right time?" Bolan asked.

"We will hear the crowds. And if you boost me up to the cell window—" he pointed to the small opening ten feet above their heads "—I can see it all."

Bolan and Jabbar talked over the details of their plan in the minutes remaining while the accused men chanted their own grief in muted tones.

Finally the guards came, two brutes twice the size of their prisoners.

The condemned men held on to the bars and screamed out their fear, their shrill pleas bouncing off the concrete walls, filling the ears of other men who knew they would probably share the same fate all too soon.

The guards clubbed the resisting fingers, crushing skin and bone, pounding their clubs on shaved heads. Finally, the battle won, the two men were dragged off to the waiting crowds.

Bolan was about to boost Jabbar to the barred window high on the wall when other guards appeared and opened the cell.

"The captain has ordered you to witness," one guard shouted at the men in the crowded cell.

Jabbar explained to Bolan. The new development changed all their plans. Maybe this was better...maybe it was worse.

"However this goes down, meet me at the parking lot at the back of my hotel tonight," Bolan whispered as they were herded out.

At first they were led in single file up several flights of stairs to the roof. Far below, the thousands of people milling about looked like ants. Their cries for blood were strident, but the words were indistinct at that distance. The two condemned men were dragged by their guards to the cobblestoned circle around the clock tower. Several of the ulema were there, old men with stringy white beards, clothed in white linen headdresses and gilt-edged robes. The Saudi executioner was a huge coffee-colored man holding a long, curved sword.

Suddenly the guards received new orders, and the prisoners were marched from the roof down the stairs.

"What is happening?" Jabbar asked one of the guards.

The uniformed men were in a festive mood. "The captain wants you up closer to the blood," the guard told him, grinning, poking him with the barrel of his rifle.

They were marched outside and pushed into a group to one side of the ulema. The condemned men had been bound hand and foot, and one had been dragged in front of the executioner. His head swung from side to side as if seeking supplication, help from someone—anyone. His eyes were wild, the frantic eyes of a cornered animal. Two men robed in black came forward and bent his head forward, exposing his neck.

The mob was in a frenzy. Two thieves had been punished before the executions. Their severed hands lay on the ground and splattered blood covered the stones in front of the man who was about to die. The locals had howled as the hands had dropped to the ground, but the foreigners in the crowd, the unbelievers, had gagged and held handkerchiefs to their mouths in horror, trying to hold back the bile that threatened to choke them.

The critical time had arrived for the first man. A blanket of silence fell over the crowd. Slowly the sword was raised. It descended in a wide arc, flashing in the morning sun, and cut through flesh and bone cleanly. The crowd screamed as one when the head dropped to the stones and rolled a few feet. Blood spurted from the stump; the body twitched. It fell to one side and was dragged away.

The guards were mesmerized. Bolan poked Jabbar in the ribs to bring him out of his stupor as he went into action. He kicked the nearest guard in the ribs and snatched his M-16 in one fluid motion. As the other guards turned, he swung the butt left and right, clubbing them senseless. He slid back the cocking lever, switched to full-auto and sprayed a burst above the heads of the men who had started to rush him. They fell to the ground, arms covering their heads.

The tall American was on the move, dodging and weaving, picking up the rifle of a fallen guard when his own weapon came up empty.

Jabbar was following his lead but not aiming high. A few prisoners and two of the ulema went down under his hail of fire.

For the Executioner it was a trade-off he had faced many times before. The lives of a few soldiers and some innocents against the safety of a nation. He had always managed to spare the innocents in the past, and he would now. He swung his weapon on the remaining guards but had no targets. The prisoners who hadn't been hit had scattered, the rest of the guards right behind them. Jabbar was nowhere in sight.

Few in the crowd had seen the action, but all had heard the shots. Everyone panicked, trampling several old men of the ulema in their haste to escape the hail of death. The Saudi executioner was down on all fours, almost impaled on his own sword. The second condemned man was rolling on the ground, trussed like a steer for branding.

Bolan dropped the rifle and melted into the crowd, ducking through an alley that led to a row of now-deserted souks that sold men's clothing. He pulled a full-length robe over his soiled clothes, selected a flowing white *guttra* and an *egal*, the black corded rings that would hold the headdress in place, then strolled out into the rushing crowds.

Not five minutes had passed since the shooting.

Police cars screamed up and down the streets, pulling people into scores of black vans. They seemed to be concentrating on Westerners. Bolan kept on walking, sometimes running, keeping in the middle of panicked crowds. He blended right in.

Batha Street was three blocks to the east and his hotel a half mile north. Every step of the way crowds flowed around him. Some found their cars and pulled frantically into traffic, their tires burning rubber. The frenzy of fear was like a fire in a theater or a dozen bulls on the loose in a crowded street. There had to be more to it than a few wild shots at the execution site. Bolan was at a loss as to what had panicked them so badly.

The hotel loomed in front of him. He kept up the same pace, entered the lobby and headed for the men's room he'd seen earlier next to the dining room. He entered a booth, pulled off the native clothes, stuffed them in a waste bin and headed for the lobby with caution.

There was no one behind the desk. In contrast to the street the lobby was like a tomb.

Bolan moved behind the desk, found a pile of police forms and riffled through them. His was there. That explained why Sedik's people weren't waiting for him at the hotel. The clerk had been lazy, slow to deliver the cards to the police. Bolan pocketed his and took off for the stairs.

THE BACK OF THE HOTEL was dark. Hundreds of mini-buses, the private livelihood of hundreds of entrepreneurs, painted as garishly as Arab imaginations would allow, sat silently in a parking lot nearby. Drivers squatted in groups, watching portable televisions set on car hoods, their coffeepots steaming over the glowing coals of smoke-dulled braziers. The night air was hot, and people still milled about. Bolan didn't know what they discussed, but they seemed more excited than he'd expected. The earlier shooting was still the topic of the day.

A dark figure sidled up to him, and Bolan reached for the knife he'd recovered from the linen room.

"Mike, it is me, Zaki."

The Sudanese was dressed in an expensive white robe and headdress. A long, black, flowing djellaba encrusted with gold braid and tied by a gold cord covered most of his robe. Such elegance was usually reserved for the rich.

"We'll talk in my room. I'm in 536. Come up in ten minutes," he told the smaller man.

Jabbar had discarded the expensive cloak when he pushed through the door a few minutes later. "They're still talking about the shooting," he said as he popped the top of a can of orange juice and sank into an overstuffed chair, his legs apart. He pulled off the *guttra* and *egal* and threw them on the floor next to him.

"You must understand, Mike. The time of the hajj is almost upon us. Millions of pilgrims will descend on the kingdom in a couple of weeks."

"I still don't get it."

"It's the Shiites, Mike. The Saudis are mostly Sunni Muslims, the predominant sect within Islam. The Shiites are more aggressive and are led by the ayatollahs of Iran."

"So the people think the Shiites were responsible for our little show?"

Jabbar sat drinking his orange juice in small sips. He sat back, his hair askew, totally relaxed for the first time since Bolan had met him. "The Saudis control Mecca and Medina, the two holiest cities of Islam. The ayatollahs are fanatics. They feel the Shiite fundamentalist approach should be spread to all Muslims, that theirs is the true word of Mohammed."

"What's happened in this feud so far?" Bolan asked.

"Recently? The worst started not long after the Iranian revolution. In 1979 a group of Shiite fanatics took over the Great Mosque of the Kabah and held it for a week."

"I remember. Didn't the Saudis execute them all?"

"Almost three hundred were killed in the fighting. More than sixty were captured alive and executed several weeks later. Every year since then the Shiites have demonstrated at the hajj, at the holiest of all Muslim ceremonies, trying to convert the hajjis to their beliefs. It is most unworthy, Mike."

Bolan sat for a few minutes and thought this through. "It's possible the Shiites killed the king and are planning to take over this year," he finally said.

"Possible, but not the only answer," Jabbar replied, preening, showing an obvious enjoyment in his present role. "The Sauds have many enemies. Their riches are beyond imagining. Someone is always plotting against them."

"But this time at least five of the brothers are dead."

Jabbar laughed. "Their father sired forty-seven legitimate sons," he said. "The younger ones are better educated. They understand the Western mind better. Maybe you have to scatter the chaff to get to the wheat."

"What is that supposed to mean?" Bolan asked.

"It means that the history of this part of the world is filled with brother killing off brother. Old Ibn Saud, their father, married and divorced almost four hundred women. He fathered more than a hundred children. Muslims are allowed to take four wives at one time if they can treat them equally. They can also divorce them for little cause. The old man married mostly for political gain. He kept them coming and going like talent on a sports team." The little man sat back and laughed at his own joke, then downed the dregs of his can of juice.

"In the last century the Rashidi tribe controlled most of the Nejd, the central plains of Arabia," he went on. "They were all-powerful and banished the forebears of the Saudis to Kuwait. Unfortunately for the Rashidis, brother killed off brother to gain power until the Rashidis were weakened beyond the ability to hold power. It's possible that they are the enemy now. But the same could be said of many other powerful tribes. The Saudis only held on to power because of the money that oil brought them. If another tribe had been in control when the money rolled in, they and not the Saudis would have ruled still."

"So you're saying the internal strife is as potent as from outside."

"Right. Our problem might be one or the other—" he paused to emphasize his point, shaking the empty can in Bolan's face "—or it could be a combination of both."

Bolan threw his empty can into a wastebasket and cursed. "This isn't exactly my specialty. How are we supposed to find out who's behind this? Sounds like a job for the CIA."

Jabbar grinned. "You forget, Mike. I am the CIA. It is a job for me."

Bolan groaned inwardly but went along. "How do you figure?" he asked.

"I find out who is responsible and you eliminate them."

"Okay. You could be right. But I don't have much money. Sedik took all the Saudi money I had, along with Connors's papers."

"That is your problem, Mike. Mine is to find out who is behind the plot."

"Good enough. I might have to call a friend for a drop."

THE ROOM LOOKED the same as it had the last time Sedik had faced his undercover men. They stood passively, but their hearts were racing as he strode to his chair on the dais and sat looking at them, his face a storm cloud.

"I am surrounded by incompetents," he shouted, pounding on the desk. It was a habit his men knew so well. It was a habit that showed when he was truly aroused. "I want that man. I want him here in the next twenty-four hours."

"He wasn't armed when we took him. Do we know if he's armed now?" one of the men asked.

"It doesn't really matter. You'll take him alive whether he's armed or not."

"He had a confederate. A Sudanese. Would the Sudanese be a better man to question?" the big man who habitually stood at the back asked. "He would be sure to tell us more."

"So you noticed the American was a warrior, Fadi. *Coward!*" he shouted. "So he's a big one and he looks like he can handle himself. No matter. We need to capture him as fast as we can. Now get out there and bring him in."

He turned to his lieutenant, knowing they would file out silently. "We need to find him," he said, his face showing the concern that only extreme pressure could produce. "He's made us look bad."

"Have you heard from the minister?" the aide asked.

"The prince is in Taif. He's keeping a low profile while his brothers are being killed off. I'm sure he won't have heard about the fiasco at the executions this morning."

The telephone rang. Both men looked into each other's eyes.

"I'm not here," Sedik said. "I'm out supervising a massive manhunt. We have a clue on the whereabouts of the American. Tell him anything that will keep him happy for a few hours."

LIEUTENANT HASSAN BINDAGII cradled the phone, his ears still ringing from the scathing denouncement he'd received from the prince who commanded the national guard. The man was one of the Saud brothers, and powerful, one of the few being considered to succeed the dead king.

Bindagii resented the dirty jobs that Sedik frequently left for him. It might be different if he was one of them. Even he didn't know why he wasn't. Since he'd been born in the town of Abha in the Southern Provinces, he's seen every kind of bribery and under-the-counter dealing. It was a way of life. But it had never been for him. Deep down he felt that it was wrong. He knew that his peers sneered at him behind his back. His wife screamed at him and demanded the same luxuries she knew the other wives enjoyed. But it just wasn't in him.

Bindagii just wanted to be the best cop that he could. He felt the money that changed hands between the merchants and the police tied their hands. Even though he received none of it, the job was compromised by the actions of those around him. Even the policies of the department were governed by the baksheesh that greased the wheels of their questionable justice.

He often examined himself as a person, held himself up against the reputation of his boss and his peers and found himself wanting. It wasn't that he didn't respect himself. It was his lack of courage that haunted him. He knew that, given the internal strength he needed, he might go his own way, be his own man. He operated within the system and instead of glorying in the profession of his choice, he was starting to hate every moment of it. The direction of his life was moving away from his objectives more every day.

As he stared at the offending telephone, he decided to change. He might not be able to make a stand during this case, it was too big and too vital to screw up. But he was going to change soon.

4

Not far from the infamous clock tower, Zaki Jabbar walked to an alley where a scribe was writing a letter for one of the many illiterates of the city. He purchased a bundle of betel twigs from a vendor, five-inch-long pieces of wood, shaved at the ends, their bark still intact. He pulled one from the bundle and started to clean his teeth with one end of the twig as others around him were doing.

It was Monday, three days after the escape. He was tired. In the past three days he had drunk mint tea in all the outdoor restaurants along Batha Street and most of the side streets leading off Batha. He was bloated, and his behind was sore from sitting. Jabbar had listened to men talk, old and young. Something every Saudi male loved to do was talk. From morning to night for three days he had talked. Or more to the point, he had listened.

They all had their theories. Shiites were coming out of the woodwork. The ayatollahs of Iran were devils who would not hesitate to kill off the ruling family to gain power over all of Islam.

Forcing himself to think about the here and now, Jabbar looked at the scribe and the betel twig seller. Their lives were uncomplicated, their choices few. Perform a service and take home a few riyals. Take advantage of a government subsidy and buy another gold band for your wife's wrist. She would be grateful for weeks.

The alley led to a small stall where a young man sold pirated tapes of the best Western music and videos. A small crowd gathered around, but Jabbar turned away. This was not the place for talk nor a likely place for reliable information on who was killing off the royal family.

He continued along the alley, which opened up on a clearing where a group of old men sat around in a circle, their *guttras* on their laps, listening to one emaciated old crone drone on, interrupted by a comment from one of his fellows from time to time.

It was an auction. Junk was piled in front of the old man in great disorder. Jabbar listened carefully. The old man was auctioning off a weather-beaten set of shutters from an ancient house. Six men bid on it. They ran the bidding from three riyals—one dollar—to twenty riyals fifty halala, almost seven dollars. The new owner would probably sell it for twenty times the price.

Jabbar sat down beside one of the old men and removed his *guttra*. Sweat streamed from his forehead, and he wiped at it with the long folds of the headdress. A tea boy rushed up, the removal of the *guttra* apparently signaling that he intended to bid. He took the glass mug of steaming tea and sat back, weary, listening amusedly to the bidding.

He bid on a couple of objects, making the first or second bid before dropping out. The old man next to him was bidding briskly, particularly on cooking pots. The heap of junk he bought was piled up behind him, where one of his sons stood dutifully.

"What do you do with all the old pots?" Jabbar asked.

"They are truly from the garbage piles of our Bedouin heritage, is it not so?" the old man cackled.

"They look like garbage," Jabbar observed.

"They are pots used by the wives and handed down from mother to daughter until they cannot be used again. Garbage. Until the Westerners came, the pots would gather dust in a junkyard in some desert town."

"They look truly ugly, old friend," Jabbar said. "Why would the foreigners buy them?"

"Only Allah knows. My sons polish them with rags until they shine," he said. "We stamp the sign of the fisherman on them, then rub the stamp with grime to make it look old. The fools think the pots date back to the days of the Christian beginnings." He chuckled through his few stubs of teeth. "The pots are copper and lead. They had brass handles and ornamentation. Junk. A beautiful way to make money, is it not?"

"But they might be sold abroad for much more," the Sudanese offered.

"Perhaps," the old man said, putting his *guttra* back on his head as the auction concluded. "But we keep raising the price and they still pay. They buy old doors and windows from the hovels of our ancestors. If the Bedouin did not piss in the desert sand, the fools would buy the pots they pissed in. It is incredible."

The others had gathered around and joined in the talk, each with a better story about the fleecing of Western matrons. "Their men come here to work and take our money. They leave the poorer for it," an old man cackled, phlegm gargling in his throat.

Jabbar looked around the group. Their faces would make a professional photographer's day, all crags and angles, the aristocracy of peninsula merchants. They appeared to house the knowledge of the ages. He sat and listened to them talk about the auction and their foolish customers, his attention wandering. He almost missed the switch to politics.

"...and he knows who is responsible. I'm sure of it."

"Who knows?" Jabbar asked.

The ancient turned his head to the Sudanese. His eyes were hooded by ridges of bone and wrinkled, hairless eyebrows. He looked like an old cobra, cold and dangerous, but too old to strike. "The sheikh of Abu Dhabi. That old bastard knows if anyone does."

"But why do you say that?" Jabbar persisted. "Why the sheikh in particular?" He paused. "What is his name?"

"He is Abdul Rachman ibn-Abdul Azziz ibn-Rashid," the old man said, looking at him as if the Sudanese were crazy. "He's a direct descendant of Ibn Rashid, the last Rashidi ruler," he went on, his face mirroring his annoyance. "Why do you doubt? We know how it is. We don't have to explain to strangers," he said, looking around at the others, receiving their unspoken agreement.

"I don't mean to offend," Jabbar replied. "But I'm appalled at the deaths of the royal princes and that no one has done anything. I may not be Saudi but I believe the Saudi tribe has done well for the kingdom."

The old man softened. "I am an unkind, thoughtless host. You will have dinner with me tonight, and we will instruct you in the ways of the peninsula Arab." He looked around at the group, smiling benevolently. "This one's education has been badly neglected," he concluded as he rose with difficulty. His son followed as the elderly man strode off with as much aplomb as his old limbs could muster.

WHILE JABBAR SAT with the old men, Bolan hot-wired a nondescript Toyota pickup and drove out to the hidden Cessna. Before he left the city he bought a pair of powerful binoculars. Taking the truck on a roundabout route, he found a butte to the north of the pesticide camp, clawed his way to the top and finally sat on the smooth rocky crest where he had a commanding view for miles around.

He couldn't see the Cessna, but he could see the deserted pesticide camp. The rows of empty metal drums were still lined up at the side of the runway. Tire tracks from police vehicles were still clear on the desert floor, leading from the camp to where he and Zaki had left the remains of the two men. No tracks led to the three buttes where the plane was hidden.

He was reasonably sure the Cessna hadn't been discovered, but he still took precautions. He drove to the back of the buttes, left the Jimmy and made his way on foot to the open area between them.

The plane sat where he had left it. He searched the ground for recent evidence of brush marks like the ones he'd made earlier to hide his tracks. He found none. No one had been there for at least four or five days.

The KX170B hummed as soon as he flipped a switch. He sought the frequency for the Dhahran Corps of Engineers base and had them on the line in minutes. He gave them a coded identification and asked for a patch to Justice and Brognola.

The radio cackled and the voice from Dhahran came back, repeated his coded identification and kept the message brief. "You're through."

"Hal? Striker. Did you get the funds?"

"I've scrounged up some. How much do you need?"

"Two hundred thousand."

"Can do. When?"

It was 1600 hours. "Make it sixteen hours—at 0800."

"We have you triangulated. Look for a chopper."

Dhahran signed off and the radio went dead. The warrior spun the dial and shut it down. As he drove back to town, he thought about the job. It was different in many ways. Saudi Arabia was like a huge prison, fortified and with excellent radar. He didn't know how Brognola was going to handle it, but he knew the big Fed would come through.

He couldn't remember when he'd had to call Brognola twice during the same job, and he had a feeling that this probably wasn't the last time.

At 0800 the next morning Bolan sat near the buttes in a fairly new Chrysler Imperial he had found abandoned on the outskirts of town the night before. The big car was one of many he'd observed gathering dust along the roadside. They appeared to be useful vehicles, but no one touched them. Their affluent owners had left them, apparently disgusted with their performance, and it was against the law to move them.

The Chrysler, maybe three years old, had been out of gas and had one spark plug fouled. Bolan expropriated the car, keeping an eye open for cruising police. He cleaned the plugs, then exchanged the car's license plates with one of the wrecks that were left in the middle of busy roads until the courts decided on settlement decrees. He had the Chrysler washed by a youth not far from his hotel, a young man who made his living with a pail of water and a dirty rag. The car looked like new.

Considering his decision to get rid of the Jimmy and his limited funds, it was a remarkable find.

It was hot. In a parked car with the windows open, it had to be a 130 degrees. The resurrected car had lost its Freon while sitting idle for so long. Even if the air-conditioning worked, Bolan couldn't keep the engine running all day. Catch-22. All he could do was wear as few clothes as possible and sweat it out.

He didn't have long to wait. At 0805 he heard the familiar sound of a chopper engine and stepped from the car. It came in from the east, probably from a carrier in the Persian Gulf. With the U.S. Navy escorting Arab tankers, they probably had no problem getting clearance for a flight to the capital.

An airman tossed something from the chopper at five hundred feet. It sailed toward him in free-fall, then was slowed by a small parachute, floating to within fifty feet of where he stood.

He didn't open the metal container until he was back in the car. Inside the box he found a shiny new attaché case stuffed with blocks of blue Saudi one-hundred-riyal bills, each bill almost equivalent to thirty-five dollars, each block worth about seven thousand. Hal had come through. Bolan knew the case contained at least the amount he had requested.

Satisfied, the Executioner drove south toward the old airport. He turned east at the road to Dhahran, Khurais Road, the car capital of the central kingdom.

Hundreds of dealer lots bordered the road a few miles out of the built-up area. Almost as many lots nearby were filled by deserted cars where owners had left them to walk to the dealers. The kingdom had no used-car market.

Bolan parked the Chrysler in the midst of some derelicts, took three blocks of money from the trunk and walked to the nearest GM dealer.

He bought a new Suburban 4WD in a matter of minutes. It was routine business for the Saudi. Bolan transferred a few blocks of blue bills to the Suburban and left the rest. If he needed them, the trunk of the Chrysler was as safe a bank as he had.

BOLAN HAD BEEN outside the hotel for an hour, and he was growing impatient. He'd just decided to go back to the room and let Jabbar find him when the Sudanese appeared beside him, all smiles.

"Did you have any luck?" Bolan asked.

"Yes. It was very satisfactory. What about you? Do we have funds?"

"We'll talk inside," Bolan said, leading the way.

Inside his room he took off the Western suit he'd purchased that day and pulled on a Saudi robe. With the air-conditioning of the hotel almost useless, it was the coolest way to go.

"Tell me about it," he said simply.

"We have to make a journey to Abu Dhabi," Jabbar said simply, beginning at the end of the story.

"Why?"

"A long story, Mike. I had dinner tonight at the home of an old man, one who has been a merchant all his life." He stopped to light a small stogie, an indulgence he permitted himself once or twice a day. Bolan took one when it was offered.

"Many other merchants, men who sell antiques, were also present. We were about twenty in number."

"Get to the point, Zaki."

"I'm just trying to emphasize the validity of my information, Mike," the Sudanese replied.

"Okay, do it your way."

The Sudanese told about his encounter at the auction and the invitation to dinner. "It was quite natural for him to invite me. It is their way. The greatest honor for a Saudi is to play the big man, the host to a group of cronies, particularly if a stranger can be impressed."

"Right. Let's hear what came out of it," Bolan said impatiently. He was starting to get itchy feet. This was definitely not his kind of game. He'd be glad when they could get into some real action.

"These old men are wise," Jabbar continued. "They know what is going on. They don't know exactly who is killing off the royal family but are sure they know one man who can tell us, if he will."

"In Abu Dhabi," Bolan said.

"You have it, Mike," the little man said.

"Who is this man? How do we get to see him?"

"He is the ruler of Abu Dhabi, Sheikh Abdul Rachman ibn-Abdul Azziz ibn-Rashid. An old and wise man."

"A Rashid? Every time we turn around we run into more Rashids."

"Patience, please, Mike. I have done my best."

"You sure the sheikh in Abu Dhabi can set us straight?"

"I am sure of it. A day or two Mike, and we will know our enemies." Jabbar smiled tentatively.

This was all wrong. They seemed to be going around in circles. He had probably done his best, Bolan thought. He mellowed. Maybe the CIA man was right.

"Okay. You got some valuable intel," Bolan finally said. He wasn't pleased at the prospect of crossing another border to see a man who probably wouldn't want to see him, but the Sudanese had at least come up with a starting point. He was right. They could probably find the Rashidi hornet's nest, but the trick was to find the people behind the deal and wipe them out.

Jabbar beamed with pleasure at the compliment. "I know Abu Dhabi. I will take you there, Mike."

"And how will you do that? It's three hundred miles to Dhahran and at least that much again to Abu Dhabi," Bolan said. "We've got to avoid Sedik and his people, so we can't take a plane. How do we do it?"

"They have built a new train line to Dhahran."

"But not to Abu Dhabi."

"No. We could take the train, then a plane. But we'd have to have an exit visa and a visa for Abu Dhabi."

"I don't like this at all."

"If we drive, I know how to get across the border without detection. We will have to get a car and—"

"I have a vehicle."

"You didn't tell me about your venture. You got the money?"

Bolan pulled a case from under the bed and flipped it open. It was half-filled with blocks of blue notes, more than fifty thousand dollars. Jabbar shouted with delight. Bolan shut him up, handed him one of the blocks and snapped the case shut.

"Is this all of it, Mike?" the Sudanese asked. "Surely there's more."

"There is, but we've got all we need for now. I've bought a new Suburban, and it can take us almost anywhere. So where do we go?"

"I know a short route. Is the Suburban one with drive on all wheels?"

"Yes."

"We drive to Al-Kharj in the southeast, then through a desert trail I know that leads to Harad, one of the busiest oil towns. We can go direct to Salwah from there. It's a town on the border of Qatar."

"I've heard we could run into desert pirates out of Qatar."

"No problem, Mike. We skirt Qatar to the south, a good road. Then back to the desert and into Abu Dhabi through the back door."

"How long?"

"In kilometers?"

Bolan shrugged. "How many hours of driving?"

"Fifteen hours if we do not stop. But we must purchase supplies first. When the souks open in the morning, we will purchase water and dried fruits, shovels and extra fuel. The desert is a cruel enemy."

5

The trip had been more tiring than Bolan expected. They crossed the border not far from the oil fields at Al-Mariyah and drove into the capital at dusk two days after their discussion at the hotel in Riyadh.

The United Arab Emirates city was like none in Saudi Arabia. It was on flat land, a giant sand spit that jutted into the Persian Gulf. The hotels that catered to foreigners were luxurious, and they didn't hold to the strict Islamic code. While sitting at a bar stool in one of the ornate hotel bars, a man could arrange for almost anything to gratify himself.

A passport wasn't needed to check into the hotel. Bolan registered in the name of Gerald Smythe. Late in the last century the British helped rid what was then the Trucial States of the Ottoman conquerors who had occupied the area for centuries, and the British still maintained excellent relations with the rulers of the seven emirates.

Jabbar understood the play all too well. He was an actor, or should have been one. When he donned the regal Arab clothes he'd purchased and got into the limousine they'd rented, he was transformed into Prince Ismad Khoweiter, the Saudi deputy minister of protocol.

"How are we going to handle this?" Bolan asked when they met in his room over a meal.

"I have had several ideas, Mike."

"Call me Smythe. Might as well start right now. Does the old man speak English?"

"He went to Oxford many years ago. You'd better be careful of any reference to England. He's sharp. And I'll call you Mr. Smythe. It is customary."

Again Bolan thought about who he was and where he was. The job had called for him to go in, find out who was knocking off the Saudi royal family and take care of them. Now he was almost a thousand miles from the Saudi capital playing games with a foreign ruler.

Things had better start going his way soon or he'd start playing by his rules. "What were those ideas of yours?" he asked impatiently.

"First, we buy something so expensive it will distract the prince initially."

"There goes my money again." Bolan grinned. The attitude of the smiling Sudanese was catching despite the situation. "You've got a one-track mind. What else?"

"We are visiting to tell him something so confidential that he will dismiss his staff and give us a private audience. It will not be easy."

"What do we tell him?"

"The Saudi royal family has been decimated. The new king will be chosen by a congress of VIPs, members of the family, ministers, the ulema, leaders of the military. The new king will be militant, one of the younger brothers. It will be a very radical choice, and the congress thought that Sheikh Rashid should be privy to the information."

"What a crock!"

"But a crock that is so flattering to Rashid that he will be blinded by pride." Jabbar laughed. "He will have his office locked and an old retainer stand guard until he calls for the door to be opened. We will have time for any kind of interrogation you wish."

JABBAR PARADED BOLAN through the gold souks, playing the role of Prince Khoweiter to the hilt. Bolan had to be impressed. Each small store was no more than twelve feet square, but each displayed millions of dollars in gold trinkets. Jabbar zeroed in on a half-dozen elaborate assemblies of chains. Each creation contained hundreds of small gold coils hanging from one thick chain large enough to span a woman's waist. In the middle of the chain the coins formed a V. A string of gold festooned with large gold coins was supposed to serve as a brassiere. The pair of precious ornaments were decorated by gold wire in filigree patterns that caught the light. Both creations were breathtaking. The whole display was the biggest collection of body ornaments Bolan had ever seen.

Jabbar explained that they were body adornment worn by a wife intent on pleasing her husband. The offerings of gold, as meager as they were, was all she wore as she plied her trade. "And this set costs only twenty thousand," he said, holding the two pieces up to the light where they spun and sparkled in his hands. "A steal."

The Sudanese had hired a local man to drive the limo and had fitted him out with new robes. With Jabbar and Bolan in the back seat, the limo pulled up at the sheikh's palace, a massive structure of pink marble. Jabbar explained that every stone had been imported from foreign quarries and brought across the sea by dhows.

The gates of the palace were opened by armed guards. They were admitted without question when Jabbar passed himself off as Prince Khoweiter.

Bolan noted that the guards were posted throughout the grounds at regular intervals and that they carried machine pistols that looked like Uzis.

"Who are the guards?" Bolan asked.

"Palace retainers who have had training. They are not from the military. They are greedy men, and lazy. It's a soft job that keeps them out of the army."

"Parasites."

"A good word, Mr. Smythe."

Jabbar and Bolan were shown up a winding staircase that led to the upper floors from a massive foyer. The old sheikh was with one of his cronies in a small room, which was guarded by an elderly man holding an ancient rifle in gnarled hands.

The room was furnished in the Arab style. Persian rugs covered the floor. Large rectangular bolsters lined the bottom of the walls, every third one placed at an angle to act as an armrest. The old men sat, legs akimbo, smoking elaborate hookahs. The pipe stands were fully four feet tall, their metal parts encrusted with semiprecious stones, and the long tubes that sucked the smoke from the smoldering pot on top, through to the purification of the water bowl at the bottom, were covered with multicolored patches of rich cloth. The soft material was encrusted with sparkling beads and sequins sewn in clusters.

The men didn't seem to be immediately aware of their visitors.

"Prince Isam Hamad Khoweiter, Saudi Arabian Deputy Minister of Protocol," the old guard announced formally in Arabic. "Mr. Gerald Smythe of the British government," he announced with less enthusiasm, using English as if he'd learned it during the past week.

The old sheikh's eyes shone, and he invited them to sit. Bolan sat in the approved fashion, an act that pleased the sheikh since most Westerners couldn't squat as easily as an Arab.

The sheikh's companion showed no signs of leaving.

"It is an honor to invite you to my humble home," Sheikh Rashid said with enthusiasm. He clapped his hands, and the inevitable tea boy set up hookahs for the newcomers, then served them mint tea.

"The Saudi royal family has asked me to deliver this gift to you," Jabbar said, unwrapping the present with a flourish.

Bolan could see the pleasure in the old man's face. One of his wives, probably still in her teens, would perform her dance of appreciation for him that night, if he was still alive to see it.

"We have been sent by the royal family," Jabbar said, "but others are involved. I regret the necessity, but what we have been asked to report is for your ears only." He looked at the other old man pointedly.

The man was insulted. Old friends were privileged to anything that went on in the household. But when the sheikh signaled to him, he pulled his old bones from the comfort of the bolsters and headed for the door.

"This is so confidential nothing must pass your lips until you hear from me again," Jabbar continued. "It would be better if you tell your guard to wait down the hall."

"Never. He has been with me since I took office," the old sheikh said indignantly. "What could be so important?"

"I am asked to discuss with you the process for selecting the next Saudi king," Jabbar said in a whisper.

"You know who he will be?" the sheikh asked excitedly. Early knowledge would permit him to set up channels for patronage before the mob descended on the new monarch.

"A radical change from the usual selection process. That is why the congress felt you should know in advance."

Sheikh Rashid clapped his hands, and the door opened. Fresh air from the hall washed over them, pushing the smoke into the far corners of the room.

"You will take up a post down the hall at least twenty paces from this door," he ordered the granite-faced old guard.

The man looked as if he'd been slapped by his sheikh, but he turned and locked the door. His footsteps could be heard padding away.

Jabbar nodded to Bolan. "Give me your knife," he said. He slid across the rugs on his haunches, then lunged forward to press the tip of the knife under the old man's chin.

"What is the meaning of this?" the outraged sheikh demanded.

"Silence! The new king will be chosen without your knowledge." Jabbar increased the pressure against the man's throat, his nose only an inch from the sheikh's. "You know who killed the king and his brothers. And you know why."

The sheikh shook his head as much as the knife would allow. Fear kept his tongue silent.

"We want to know who is responsible for killing off the royal family. We want to know who they are and where they are."

Again the old man shook his head. "They will kill me," he said, his words garbled by a tongue paralyzed with fear.

"You will die anyway," Jabbar returned, turning the knife in his hand, tracing the dull edge back and forth over the man's withered skin.

"Hail," the sheikh croaked.

"What does he mean?" Bolan asked.

"Hail. A town. Maybe three hundred miles north of Riyadh," the Sudanese explained.

"What about the place?"

"I told you about the people there. Hail is the seat of Rashidi power. Maybe they've finally decided to try to take over again."

"The Rashidi-Saudi feud?" Bolan asked.

"They've been at it for hundreds of years."

"Is that it?" Bolan asked. "Are your relatives getting ambitious again?"

The sheikh glowered at them with hate-filled eyes. "They will get you. They will hear about my shame and they will hunt you down," he spit, his chest heaving as he spoke. He was flushed and hyperventilating.

"Someone else has to be in this with the Rashidis of Hail. They don't have the money or the men," Jabbar said.

"Let's keep it moving," Bolan said to Jabbar.

"Who's in this with them?" Jabbar persisted, threatening with the knife. The CIA man followed the traditions of his family. Old people in the tribe were revered. He hated to take on an old man like this, but this was no time to let down. The man might not be able to match him in strength, but he'd have them both killed in a second if he got free. He might even be in this with his cousins.

"Powerful friends," the sheikh ground out, his throat constricted. "They'll squash the Saudis and they'll kill you for this."

"Who are they?" Bolan demanded. "Russian?"

"You'll never know from me," the sheikh said. He looked as if he were about to faint. "My people have many friends, just as you have many enemies. Your enemies are their friends."

As Jabbar held him by the head and prepared for the final question, the old man's eyes widened as if he were in pain. He took one deep, gasping breath and shouted in agony, slumping into the cushions.

As the ancient retainer burst into the room, Bolan pulled his silenced Beretta and put a slug through the man's temple.

It was too late now for recriminations. They didn't have much information, but it was enough to take them to the next step. Bolan ran to the door and chanced a cautious look into the hallway. Guards at each end of the hall still manned their posts. Apparently they hadn't heard the sheikh cry out.

6

Scant seconds after Bolan and Jabbar left the room, they heard a scream behind them from the tea boy. The guards in the hallway leveled their machine pistols. Bolan took one man out of the play with a quick head shot, but Jabbar was slower. His handgun clattered to the floor as he took a half-dozen 9 mm slugs in the chest.

The noise was earsplitting in the confined space. A stream of manglers from Bolan's Beretta punched the second guard backward, his Uzi spitting tumblers wildly at seven hundred rounds a minute.

The gunfire reverberated and died. The hallway stank of cordite. The Executioner took one look at the mangled body of Jabbar and headed for the stairs and the front door, pursued by excited voices shouting Arabic. The household was totally alert and preparing for battle.

Bolan only had his Beretta, so as he passed a dead guard, he scooped up an Uzi and pulled two extra clips from the guy's belt. Two guards appeared at the foot of the stairs. Bolan beat the first to the draw with three 9 mm slugs in the chest, but the other guy got lucky. A shot from his subgun creased the Executioner's shoulder before he shot a burst into the guard's gut.

Bolan's arm was numb, and a quick look at the wound in his shoulder told him that he'd gotten off easy this time. He drew the Beretta with his right hand, held it with his left and shoved the Uzi into his belt.

The massive front doors stood open. Men out in the courtyard were shouting commands. Feet scuffled back and forth along the corridors nearby. Bolan waited a few seconds to try to learn the strength of his enemy, but it was useless. He charged the rest of the way, caught four guards in a circle, talking wildly, gesticulating.

Firing with the gun in his left hand, he treated each to a dose of death as he raced for the rented limousine.

The vehicle was pointed in the wrong direction. He couldn't turn the damned thing and make it to the huge steel gates before the rest of the Rashidi guards closed in. The driver Jabbar had hired came on the run and was cut down from behind.

Bolan spotted an old Jeep close to the front door, and slugs kicked up the dirt close to his heels as he dived for the vehicle. The keys weren't in the ignition. A volley shattered the windshield, shards of glass spraying the front seat as he searched the sun visor then under the seat for the keys.

He found them on the floor. The Jeep roared to life.

The massive steel gates were starting to close automatically. The electric controls gave the gates an even but slow pace. Gunfire tore at the roof of the Jeep as Bolan raced to the gates, the sides of the old vehicle nearly scraped off as it forced its way through.

He was out.

On the streets every face was turned to the careering vehicle.

So where was he heading? Bolan had to get rid of the easily identifiable Jeep. He couldn't buy a car, though he had enough money in his pockets. He just wasn't prepared to spend it all on new transport.

Bolan heard sirens far behind and tore into a large parking lot outside a mosque and drove the Jeep into the middle of the parked cars.

He searched ten cars before he found one with the keys in the ignition, an old Mercedes 300SE. He reversed it out of the lot and drove back toward the palace. An Arab headdress was on the seat beside him, and he stopped for a few seconds to put it on and adjust the long folds of cloth across and over his shoulders before taking off again at a stately pace.

Official cars raced past him, sirens screaming. He took a circular road that skirted the city, driving within the speed limit. They hadn't set up roadblocks yet, but they would soon. When the police finally stopped panicking and began to get organized, he would be in real trouble.

Bolan made an inventory of his assets. He still had the Uzi and perhaps forty rounds. The Beretta still held several rounds, and he had one spare clip. The commando knife remained in its sheath and might be useful.

While he concluded the inventory of his weapons, he spotted a field on the outskirts with his peripheral vision. He made a U-turn and went back to check it out. It was a small airfield that contained one lone plane, a Gulfstream. It looked a little worse for wear, probably one of the first Model III's to come off the assembly line in 1979 or 1980.

Better than nothing. It was all he had at the moment. As he drove through the gates, two guards, attracted to the fence by the goings-on in the city, turned to the car, weapons raised.

Bolan slipped from the seat, the Uzi up and ready. When the door swung clear, he got off two short bursts. The men flew back to the fence and lay still, their bodies partially hidden in tall grass.

It was early evening, the sun still well above the horizon to the west. Bolan ran for the boarding ladder amidships, then made his way to the cockpit.

Controls filled most of the forward bulkhead and the two sides of the cabin. He slid into the left seat and flipped on the power switches, taking time to read the English markings carefully.

Without an external power source, Bolan pressed the starter button for the port engine. The internal batteries were low. The starting motor ground over slowly, complaining, refusing to kick over.

Then it fired. He revved the plane up and let it idle while he tried the same routine with the starboard engine, which refused to fire. He could see a convoy of flashing lights along the road leading to the field. They'd be on him in a moment.

The batteries turned over the starboard engine slowly. It was hell. Maybe he'd have to take the crate up on one engine, but he didn't want to try.

The other engine fired and began to rev to full power. He checked the starboard mirror and saw a cloud of blue smoke spew out along the tarmac.

Bolan held the control bar in his left hand, eased the throttles forward with his right and released the brakes. His shoulder screamed at him as the pain tore down his arm.

The police cars had rounded the perimeter of the field and were through the gates. The Gulfstream fishtailed right and left as the Executioner tried to remember how to control turns while taxiing.

The plane crossed over a grass verge between runways and was finally on smooth concrete. Bolan didn't have time to check the wind direction. He pushed the throttle to full power and held the control bar steady, ready to pull back when the engines were at full revs.

In a few seconds he pulled back on the bar. The lift he should have felt wasn't there. The wind direction was on his tail, and he was running out of runway. The cavalcade of cars and trucks, filled with Arabs who were firing wildly, followed him down the ribbon of concrete.

To hell with it. He'd had enough of cat and mouse. He kicked her to starboard, toward the sea. The odds favored an offshore breeze.

The jet began to lift, shakily at first but with gathering speed. Bolan could feel the plane fight him. The air lift wasn't even. It was choppy, making the craft yaw from side to side as it tried to angle into a climb.

He brought the jet around to seaward a few more degrees, and it smoothed out. The first battle had been won.

THE MISSILE FRIGATE cruised at twenty knots a few miles southeast of Bahrain. She had been a factor in sinking one Iranian gunship two days earlier and rounding up a half-dozen others ships that had been laying mines in the shipping lanes leading to Bahrain and Kuwait.

For the past five seconds Signalman First Class Bates had been following an unidentified bogey heading out to sea from Abu Dhabi. He checked the log of flight plans provided by the Saudi Arabian air control at Dhahran. No match. He signaled his lieutenant.

"Unidentified bogey at two-sixty degrees ten miles out of Abu Dhabi, sir. She's making a wide sweep, heading for the mainland again."

"On the log?" the lieutenant asked.

"No, sir."

The lieutenant didn't hesitate. They'd had too many close calls lately. He flipped a switch and was talking to Dhahran in seconds. "This is the frigate *Francis Scott Key*. We have an unidentified aircraft over Abu Dhabi at five thousand feet heading inland."

An American voice answered from Gulf Control at Dhahran. "We have her on scope. The Saudis are scrambling two from Al-Kharj. Estimate contact in ten minutes."

"Roger and out," the lieutenant replied. "Nice work, Bates." He touched his man on the shoulder. "Let's keep those bastards as far from this tub as possible."

"I'm with you, sir."

THE OFFICE WAS almost dark. Only one light was lit, a lamp standing on one corner of the desk that shone on the piles of paper that habitually piled up on the captain's desk.

A red-and-white checked *guttra* was draped on the chair beside Sedik. He looked weary as he went over the papers that seemed to make a jailer of him each night. His new wife, the young Egyptian he had met and married a year earlier, would be waiting. She was a passionate woman, always impatient that he had to spend every second night with his first wife.

Suddenly something interesting caught his eye. He sat up and stared at the thin sheet of typed Arabic script in front of him. It had been forwarded to him as a matter of routine from the UAE police on their teletype network earlier that day.

An American posing as a British envoy from the Saudi royal family was permitted entry to the palace in Abu Dhabi today. The intruder murdered Sheikh Abdul Rachman Rashid and several of his guards. The killer escaped, but his accomplice was killed by the palace guards. It is reported that the dead man spoke Arabic with the accent of an East African. At this reporting he has not been identified. An hour after the assassination an executive jet was stolen from a private airfield. It is assumed that the two incidents were connected.

"It was the American!" Sedik shouted to an empty office. The dead man was the Sudanese. He *knew* the American was his man. But what was he doing in Abu Dhabi? Why would he pose as a representative of the royal family and have a private interview with the sheikh who ruled a neighboring state?

Maybe he was being paranoid, Sedik thought. At least forty thousand Americans lived in his kingdom at the last count. So why did it have to be the one he sought?

The door opened, spilling light from the hall, and Lieutenant Bindagii entered the room. In the half-light his features were barely discernible.

"You've been catching up, too?" Sedik asked.

"Too much paper. The world revolves around it," Bindagii replied. He was obviously tired. He carried his *guttra* in one hand, the ends dragging on the floor, a sure sign of fatigue in an otherwise scrupulously fastidious man.

"Look at this," Sedik suggested, holding out the report from Abu Dhabi.

The paper had the same effect on Bindagii. "It's him!" he declared.

"Either it is, or we're both paranoid," Sedik said wearily. "I'm chasing ghosts by this time. Why would he be there?"

"Why does he do anything?" Bindagii asked. "I think it's him, and we should do something about it."

"What the hell do we do? Tell me that. You can read," Sedik said. "He stole a private jet and took off. He could be anywhere within three thousand miles by now."

"I'll call the air base at Al-Kharj," Bindagii suggested, picking up the phone.

Sedik took it from him and put it down. "You forget, Hassan. Prince Abdullah is not speaking to Prince Sultan. Members of the national guard do not talk to the air force. Petty jealousies. They're both jockeying for appointment as our new king."

"Damned politics," Bindagii said. "You're saying that the air force won't tell me if they have a plane on their scopes?"

"You learn quickly, Lieutenant. Welcome to the club," Sedik said, opening a file on the American and placing the report from the UAE inside.

BOLAN MADE A SHAKY TURN, lost some altitude and started to head inland. At three thousand feet he passed over the harbor. The desolation of the desert was below him in seconds, shutting out all signs of life.

He checked the altimeter. At twenty-five hundred feet he leveled out. He wanted to take her down on the deck, but he didn't feel secure enough at the controls. This wasn't a Cessna. He'd only have to make a minor mistake at one hundred feet to plow up a mile of sand dunes.

The decision came to him at the moment he pictured himself and the jet breaking up. It came to him in the grinning face of Jack Grimaldi. He'd give anything if the flying wizard was sitting at the controls and he was relaxed in the right seat. Maybe he could do something about that.

While he was in level flight, Bolan checked for maps. He found only one in a pocket on the left of the pilot's seat. While he glanced at it, he saw a small forest of oil rigs to port.

According to his map, it had to be Al-Idd. He was heading too far south. He corrected to 225 degrees and headed for the oasis at Al-Ubayla. He had to be over the middle of the most feared desert in the world, but at least he was heading for a known watering spot. If his fuel held out, he had one-quarter of the plane's capacity, he'd at least make it to the oasis. One step at a time. If he made it that far, he'd try for one of the bigger towns. He still had resources. The rest of his cash still sat in the trunk of the Chrysler near the Khurais auto marts. He thought of Grimaldi again. He could call Brognola....

His mind had been wandering. Two shapes appeared at the outer edges of his vision and moved forward to fly parallel with him.

They were the most beautiful aircraft he had ever seen. The forward bubble allowed vision in every direction, and he could see the pilot of each aircraft clearly.

F-16s. The deadliest fighters in the world. He looked them over as they slowed to cruise with him at about five hundred miles per hour.

They were armed for war. Two Sidewinders were attached to each wing tip; cluster bombs hung under each wing closer to the fuselage; long-range fuel tanks were suspended even closer to the fuselage, and between them he recognized a data processing pod.

One of the pilots signaled him to descend. He shrugged his shoulders. Where the hell could he land? The other pilot pointed to his earphones. Bolan found a throat mike and earphones, put them on and swung the radio dial from end to end, trying to pick them up. Everything he heard was Arabic—they were Saudi pilots.

He'd assumed they were Americans. He'd been mistaken, and it might cost him his life. Just because he'd heard some commands in English from the navy in the Gulf when he'd plugged in earlier, why did he have to assume the pilots were American?

Bad news. The Saudi air force had shot down two Iranian fighters over their territory the previous week. They didn't know who he was. He had markings and they could check the ownership. By now the Gulfstream had probably been reported stolen. And by someone who had just murdered the ruler of Abu Dhabi. They had to think of him as a terrorist or a Shiite fundamentalist. Either way, he was an enemy and he was going down.

One of the pilots signaled him to follow. One fell in at his stern and the other took a position in front. They began a wide turn to the north. North was Riyadh. They were probably from the base at Al-Kharj. No way was he going to follow. Once they had him on the ground he'd be a dead man.

He pushed the control bar forward, kicked a rudder and peeled off to port, due west.

They didn't hesitate. The lead plane pulled straight up and disappeared. The other was on his tail.

He was down to one thousand feet when he saw a missile streak from the F-16 on his tail. He made a desperation turn, and the Sidewinder plowed into a dune ahead of him. The jet had been too close. The pilot wouldn't make the mistake again. He'd either blow Bolan out of the sky with cannon fire or drop back and fire another missile.

The warrior heard the explosion, felt the ship shudder and in his port mirror saw an engine disintegrate. Cannon fire had torn it apart. The Saudi aircraft continued to fire, stitching large holes in the wing in a line toward the cabin.

The Gulfstream began to yaw to starboard as it lost weight. The engine was gone, the wing about to fold and fire trailed along the side of the fuselage from torn fuel lines.

Bolan yanked at the landing-gear controls. The electrical system still worked. He expected the cannon fire to reach him all the time he fought the controls to bring the jet level.

He didn't know which way the wind was blowing. All he could see were giant dunes for miles in every direction. Not one flat spot broke the undulating landscape.

He gave the craft full flaps and tried to compensate for the lost engine. At one hundred feet he was coming in at more than three hundred klicks, and he knew he was going to buy it.

The weakened wing broke loose, and the jet swung to port. It missed the top of a dune, but slammed into the next and flipped, the craft turning nose over tail, kicking up sand, spewing smoke and raw fuel in its wake.

At last the Gulfstream lost its momentum and broke up, rolling partway down the giant dune and coming to rest in a gully of sand.

Bolan had been belted in and had escaped serious injury. He was disoriented, and all that he was aware of at the moment was that the motion had stopped. He popped his seat belt, crawled to one of the fissures in the fuselage and dropped to the ground just as the aircraft exploded.

The F-16s flew a pattern over the pall of smoke for ten minutes then radioed to Dhahran. "Central control, Red Leader. The bogey is on the ground, burning."

"Any survivors?"

"I do not think so," the flight leader reported. "It doesn't matter if anyone survived. The wreck is in the middle of the Rub' al-Khali. He couldn't walk clear for more than two miles."

"Repeat. Did anyone survive?"

"No, sir. No survivors."

"Break off. Well done, Red Leader."

BOLAN LAY ON HIS SIDE fifty yards from the burning wreck. He rolled over and shaded his eyes from the sun, which seemed like a torch in the sky. Smoke swirled in every direction. The mission a success, the two fighters had returned to base.

Nearly a half hour had passed before the Executioner stirred and began a systematic search for salvage. Already the sun had taken its toll. He felt dehydrated.

The search, one circuit of the plane, Bolan painfully dragging one foot after the other, didn't produce much. Everything that wasn't burned was scattered in the sand. The debris was mostly cushions and rugs. He found one half-filled bottle of water, the most precious commodity. The Uzi had disappeared, but he still had his own weapons and a pocketful of money.

His injured shoulder was covered with sand. The wound throbbed but the pain was bearable. The biggest problem was keeping flies from it. Where the hell did they come from miles from nowhere?

So this was it, the big man thought. After hundreds of battles around the world, the Executioner was going to spend his last hours with his back on the desert floor staring up at a ball of fire.

No way. He wasn't about to give in. He'd survived a desert trek before. He'd give it his best shot now. The warrior decided to head in the direction of Al-Ubayla. He took a bearing on the sun and started up the first dune away from the wreckage.

THE COMPOUND WAS one of the largest in Hail. Inside its massive walls the eight houses were identical. Each contained more than a dozen rooms, including separate quarters for the women and the servants. In the middle of the compound one building, squat and square, served as a meeting house. The whole setup was drab, the color of the dunes in the nearby An-Nafud, as if the occupants were disinterested in appearances, preoccupied with their work and not its rewards.

The compound stood apart from the rest of the community. If one had no business there, one avoided it.

The residents knew the power of the Rashid brothers, who were the sons of old Ibn Rashid and the underground rulers of the northern part of the Saudi kingdom. They had the loyalty of most of the local people, but they governed by fear. Men of the region visited when summoned. They obeyed but they did not volunteer.

It was late in the day. The evening meal had been taken in the home of the eldest brother, and later they had adjourned to their mosque for evening prayers and finally to their pipes.

As was the custom, the women and children had squatted before the same pile of lamb and rice after the men had eaten. Later the servants had eaten the remaining scraps before they had cleared the dishes away. Now, as the moon tried to bend its light into the heart of the meeting house, the brothers sat with their hookah pipes, filled the room with acrid smoke and talked.

Arab men loved to talk. They especially loved to talk about their trips abroad, the women they had charmed, the gambling tables they had looted. The Rashid brothers were not as garrulous as their kind. They had inherited a deep-seated hatred of the Saudi rulers. Their ancestors had ruled in centuries past and they felt that it was their right. But it was a right dictated by force. They had not been able to muster sufficient force to take the struggle forward until now.

"We heard from Abu Dhabi this afternoon," the eldest brother began, his tone sad. He was Hussein, a big man who was tormented by his heritage and the hand that had been dealt to him. He was dressed in a startlingly white *thobe* with a four-button collar and French cuffs. Gold studs served as buttons up the front of the garment and at his neck. Diamond-encrusted cuff links shone from his wrists. His *guttra* was of fine blue-and-white-checked material, which was distinctive to the Rashidis. The brothers had adopted the unusual color, following the lead of the old patriarch, their father, who had lived well past eighty and guided his people with a strong hand for more than fifty years.

"Abdul Rachman is dead," he continued. "A Sudanese and an American posing as a Briton killed him."

"The assassins were killed by the palace guard?" a younger brother asked.

Hussein's eyes raked the group, making sure he had their attention. "The Sudanese, but not the American. He escaped to an airport and stole a private jet."

"The Saudis will have shot him down," another brother offered.

"Don't be sure," Hussein said. "We take nothing for granted."

"Do we know what the American wanted with our cousin?" Hamza, the youngest man in the room, asked.

"Yes," Hussein replied. He had been waiting for the question. "The American was asking about us, where we lived, who were our allies."

"He is after us?"

"Who is he? Who sent him?"

The brothers started to speak at once, all asking their own questions.

"Silence!" Hussein shouted into the wall of sound. "You are like old women," he chided them. "What would you ask, young Hamza?"

"If Abdul Rachman is dead, who passed the word to us?"

"Intelligent question, as usual." Hussein grinned. He shared his late father's affection for the young man. "They were alone. A guest had been excused. Most unusual. The guard had been dismissed on the pretext that the infidel's news was of the greatest importance."

"So what—?" Hamza started to interrupt.

Hussein held up a hand and gazed around the group, knowing that he had their complete attention. "The sheikh, our illustrious old cousin, recorded all his conversations. Many men have told him things they have later regretted."

He waited, drawing smoke through the long colorful tube of his hookah, listening to the water bubble, feeling the smoke at the back of his throat. "Abdul Rachman's people pieced it together this way. The intruders demanded to know about us and our allies. Our cousin went to the arms of Allah, telling the two invaders he would never reveal one word that would hurt us."

The room was silent until Hamza spoke again. "Our cousin was a hero, a man among men. But this man, this American, he is dangerous. I don't think he is dead, and we should prepare for him."

Hussein beamed at the younger man. "As usual you are right. We must prepare for him. He must never learn who our allies are. Not until after the hajj."

"By then it will be too late for him," Hamza said.

"Exactly."

The big middle-aged man looked at his brothers, seven pairs of eyes returning his fiery gaze. They were united, and this time they would win.

HAMZA RASHID WAS a small man compared to Hussein. He was small in stature but not in the regard of his brothers. Of them all, he was the only one who had been educated in the West. He knew how the infidels thought, how they regarded the peninsula Arab, how ignorant they were of the inner workings of a tribe like his.

The will to conquer had burned in him since the days when he sat at his father's knee as a small child while evening campfires burned and men spoke of the past. They had ruled the whole peninsula in centuries past. It had been their right. It still was.

Hamza was a lot closer to an understanding of the foreigners than they were of his people. He had seen the stock markets in action, the frenetic rush to succeed that permeated Madison Avenue. He had been taken to small towns in America, and he understood their attitudes, or he understood how they had originated. They felt that it was their God-given right to enjoy an affluent life-style while half the world starved. Yet they could not understand, and opposed the right of his people to take back what was theirs.

And he understood why they opposed him and his people. If the Rashidis took back what was rightfully theirs, the control of Gulf oil would be in their hands, and the hands of those who supported them.

They looked down on his people as enemies of society. Whose society? Not the Arab society. Westerners didn't understand the Arab mind and they never would. They were blinded by their own need to maintain the status quo.

But for now he had to face a lone American, a representative of the overlord, a killer sent to thwart their cause.

He wouldn't.

He couldn't.

They and their allies were waiting, and they were capable of sending the Western assassin to perdition with the devil whose enclave was quickly becoming filled with the products of Western greed and avarice.

All he wanted was what was naturally his, what Allah had decreed for him. He had been born to it. He had lived all his life to fulfill it.

It was going to happen.

7

The sun was consuming Bolan. Just lying at the top of the dune was like lying in a giant oven, trying not to look at the oven light. Someone had turned the temperature to the end of the dial and put in a two-hundred-watt bulb instead of a fifteen. It seemed as if it were two inches from his eyeballs.

His meager water supply had run out. He had tried to ration it, to take it a few drops at a time, but the supply was too small to last long. The warrior's lips were cracked, his tongue swollen and his exposed skin burned.

How many hours? He hadn't checked the time when he'd started to stagger up one dune and down the next. All he could see for miles around was sand in great undulating dunes and a line of footprints like a miniature zipper that told the world that he had passed this way. His tracks would last until the next sandstorm, but there was a real possibility that he wouldn't.

He knew the drill as well as anyone alive. Stay with the wreck. If he'd stayed, the Saudis would probably follow up on their kill. But the trail he left made the whole play useless. Anyone could follow it. He'd hoped for a wind to cover his tracks and some form of habitation before now. But it wasn't going to happen.

He thought about the conversation with Brognola in the diner back in Washington, and he smiled humorlessly at this last bit of irony. The effort just opened more cracks in his parched lips. Persistent flies buzzed around the moisture that oozed from the cracks. Hal had told him that he would be alone on this one. He'd been so right.

This was as alone as a man could get.

How long had it gone on? He'd seen camels and trucks heading his way in the past half hour, yet when they got close they would disappear in the waves of heat that blurred his vision.

Another truck came at him out of the haze, another vision that would fade as it got closer. This one was the most realistic yet, containing both sound and faces—the sound of men speaking in Arabic; the faces of men who looked concerned. The three wise men looking for a messiah.

But the vision didn't disappear. A man held a goatskin to Bolan's lips and washed his face with the cool liquid. They spoke to him in rapid Arabic. When their queries drew no response, one man ventured a sentence in halting English.

"You are British?" the Bedouin asked.

"American," Bolan rasped. He noted the soiled robes, the black-and-white checked *guttras*, the hawklike features, the old Lee-Enfield rifles slung across their shoulders. These were desert Bedouin who would know nothing of his recent activities, as they avoided officialdom as much as he.

"We saw smoke," the man continued. "We found the burned airplane. You should have stayed with it. If storm come, you disappear."

Bolan ignored the remark. "You're camped near here?" he asked, his throat feeling better. He reached for the goatskin and took more liquid, slowly, letting it trickle down his throat, washing his lips with his tongue to soften them.

"Two hour. Maybe more. We take you there."

They lifted the warrior with the bed of the old Toyota pickup. He was surprised at how weak he was.

On the way to the camp the Arabs chatted among themselves. They had noted the Beretta and the knife but had said nothing. Each man wore a curved sword in a jeweled scabbard, and each had a rifle. Apparently an armed man was not an oddity in this hostile environment.

The first Bolan saw of the camp was a V -shaped outcropping of rock that rose more than four hundred feet off the desert floor. A dozen tents made of goatskins were pitched in the lee of the wind, scores of conventional tents fanning out around the traditional ones.

Barking dogs rushed to the truck; women turned away and donned their veils; children approached on the run, their happy voices like music to the ears of the warrior.

They led him, still groggy, to the shade of a tent. A woman hurried forward, carrying a plate of bread and cheese. Her dark eyes regarded him for a moment, then she stared shyly at the ground.

The adults of the camp were curious about him, but they kept their distance. He knew something of the Bedouin. They were friendly and generous, but they were shy. He wondered if they knew what was going on in their kingdom, that the royal family was being decimated.

An old man finally came to stand in front of him. He nodded. "I will sit with you," he said in perfect English.

Bolan gestured to one of the many cushions beside him.

"I am Amer Ezzedine al-Murra," the slight man said. His hawklike features could have graced the walls of a national gallery. He carried himself like an aristocrat.

"My name is Mike Ford. I'm an American."

"We are well-disposed to Americans, Mr. Ford. The al-Murras and the Saudis have long been grateful for your technical skills and your military advice."

The short speech told Bolan many things. The soldier wasn't a historian, but he'd done his homework on the flight to London. The old man had used Bolan's last name, so he had probably been Western-educated. He was an al-Murra, from the cream of Bedouin manhood and a tribe friendly to the royal family. His tribe had been one of the first to ride with the patriarch Ibn Saud, the father of the reigning Saud brothers, when he had left his exile in Kuwait to take back the kingdom from the Rashidis.

At first it occurred to Bolan to reveal his mission to this honorable ally of the Saud family, but he held back. It would be typical of them to ride into Riyadh in force and make a show of strength that would be useless against the hidden enemy.

"My President is well-disposed to the royal family. I was on a mission on his behalf when my plane crashed."

"You will note that we are well equipped here." Al-Murra pointed to the two massive tanker trucks parked not far away from a small fleet of pickup trucks. A Mercedes limousine was parked alongside, its white paint gleaming in the sun.

"One of the tankers has water, the other gasoline," al-Murra explained. "We have electric generators and a powerful shortwave radio. We are not the ignorant Bedouin of the books you read," he said, a faint smile creasing his parchment skin. "We are curious why you were flying a jet owned by an Abu Dhabi oil man and shot down by the Saudi air force."

Bolan sipped the mint tea that one of the women had brought. He stalled, not knowing how to answer. The one thing that he found strange was that no one had taken his gun away. What was their game?

"We also know that the sheikh of Abu Dhabi was killed just before the jet was stolen. Was that your work, Mr. Ford?"

The old man looked at him with eyes that didn't waver. The eyes of a viper. Eyes that could look at one of his people, demand the truth and get it.

"Has your radio told you about your friends, the Saudi royal family?" he asked.

"We mourn their passing. They have been accepted into the bosom of Allah, the merciful."

"I'll tell you the truth," Bolan said. What choice did he have? He was hundreds of miles from the nearest town and without transport. He didn't even have his full strength and probably wouldn't be himself for days.

"Let me tell you part of it first," the old man interrupted. "You are close to the American President. He sent you here, one man, to find out who is killing off our royal family."

"How do you—"

"What I don't understand is why one man? Are you so skillful you can do what the national guard and the CID cannot do?"

Bolan decided to hold his tongue. He'd be better off listening than talking at this point.

"Allah is close to me. Through him I know about you, Mr. Ford," al-Murra went on. "I do not know all, but I know you are a man who can help if anyone can. Are you surprised?"

"I haven't had much experience with psychics, and most of what I've heard I haven't believed."

"Most people would agree with you. It is difficult to explain. It is partly vision and partly common sense," the old man said, sipping his mug of tea. "My people found you near the wrecked aircraft. You are armed. You obviously killed the hated Abdul Rashid. What took you to him? Why are you in the kingdom in the first place? The mind seeks answers. Some of the answers come as pure logic, some helped by the love of Allah."

"You people don't have to get involved in this."

"We are loyal to our own, Mr. Ford, and must do what is right and just. I will give you my eldest son. I have been pondering how to help these past days. Your arrival is timely."

This was just great, Bolan thought. All he needed was the old man's favorite son to trip over his feet and get himself killed. When he got back to Riyadh, he'd planned on calling Brognola and getting him to parachute Grimaldi in. He didn't want to go all the way on this one alone. Jack Grimaldi would be a great solution. Still, neither of them spoke the language fluently.

Al-Murra clapped his hands, and an old woman came forward and bent her ear to his mouth. She shuffled off.

A man about Bolan's age strode into the tent and stood in front of his father. Tall with broad shoulders, he was dressed in an elaborate robe. His piercing black eyes bored into Bolan, but he said nothing. It was as if he were reporting to his commanding officer. His posture was parade rest.

"This is my son Adnan. This man is Mr. Mike Ford," he told his son. "Sit with us. We will plan what must be done."

That's all he needed, Bolan thought. In the middle of the Rub' al-Khali, the Empty Quarter, a tribal chief, a psychic, was going to tell him how to complete his job.

"Don't sweat it, soldier," Adnan said, taking a seat in front of them. "My father knows the score."

Bolan almost choked on his tea. The younger al-Murra grinned. His face was handsome and rugged, and under the native robe Bolan suspected he carried a powerful body.

"Why did you call me 'soldier'?" he asked.

"Takes one to know one." The reply was crisp, the accent slightly British. "Sergeant Adnan al-Murra, Twenty-second Special Air Services Regiment out of Bradbury Lines, retired. Been in and out of Burma and Malaysia cleaning out the rebels. Fought alongside the Bérets Rouge in Corsica and the Sarawak Rangers in Borneo. A long time ago," he concluded, picking a date from a tray brought by one of the women. "I was at Bradbury Lines the same time as your Charlie Beckwith. I was just a kid. I may be a little rusty now, but you never forget, right?" He ended the recital by pulling a sand-colored beret from a pocket and replacing his desert headdress with it. With the well-worn beret and the lean, hard jaw, he looked as if he'd been born to the military.

Bolan grinned at him. Here was the kind of man the CIA needed in place on a permanent basis if his head wasn't muscle-bound by military protocol.

The Executioner wasn't about to recite his exploits—they might be hard to explain. But he needed this man, a man who had trained with the American officer who originated the American Delta Force and based it on the SAS. There was no question he could use him.

"Why aren't you still with the SAS or someone else?" Bolan asked.

"Family," al-Murra said. "The SAS causes weren't mine. I fought in some of the African coups, helped oust Amin, but my heart wasn't in it. Family, Mr. Ford. In Saudi Arabia the sons live with the father until he dies. The eldest usually becomes the new patriarch. The other sons take off to found their own colonies. But we all stay close."

"We could use some of your family thinking. Seems our families are falling apart."

"We also have Allah. God and family. The bonds are very strong."

"What made you leave the family in the first place?"

"Hot blood. My grandfather rode out of Kuwait with Ibn Saud back in 1902. My father rode with them in the campaigns of the thirties. I had to get out and prove myself."

"How strong are the bonds between the Saudis and the al-Murras?" Bolan asked.

"Words are inadequate," the elder al-Murra broke in. "As my son told you, my father rode with Ibn Saud. I, too, was privileged to be a part of history. I knew the father of our country. He was like an uncle to me."

"Do the Saudis share your feelings?" he asked.

"Yes," Adnan answered for his father. "The older ones treat my father as an honored friend. They are available to him at all times."

"And the young ones, the young sons?" Bolan asked.

"My friends," Adnan replied. "Still, we do not know every one intimately. One might be behind the plot, one we don't know."

"You might be right. But I believe the Rashidis of Hail are the front men," Bolan said.

"The front men, Mr. Ford?" the senior al-Murra asked. "You think a third party is involved?"

"I'm sure of it."

"The sheikh of Abu Dhabi?" the old man pressed.

The man was sharp, Bolan thought. He could see that they could be the best of allies, not men to fool with. In their dealings he would have to be up front all the way. "I don't kill helpless old men. When I left Abdul Rachman, he had collapsed. It's possible that he had a heart attack. He told us that the Rashidis had powerful allies, but he passed out before he could explain. I didn't have time to wait for the answer."

"Things must have been hot at the palace," Adnan said. "We heard you lost a companion."

"A good man."

"And now you're alone?" the old man asked.

"For the time being."

"My son will help you, but first you should tell us who you really are."

The statement didn't come entirely as a shock. The clues all pointed that way. Why would he use his real name in this job? The old man might be psychic, but this question was based on pure logic.

He decided not to play games. If they were going to be honest with him, he'd return the favor. "The name's Mack Bolan. It won't mean anything to you."

"Oh?" Adnan said. "Ever hear of Mad Dog Bates?"

"Sure. A broker of mercenaries."

"When I left the SAS, I fought alongside him a couple of times. A real rough type. You know what it's like in the military. We had time to sit around between firefights. We talked of other men who got into international action, and your name came up."

Bolan's curiosity was aroused. He had to know what the younger al-Murra knew if they were to work together. "What was the story?"

"A good fighting man who was shrouded in mystery. He thought you were covert, but not tied into the CIA."

"I know of him, but we don't know each other." Bolan had made up his mind that he'd use al-Murra. He didn't want to go near the royal family, to use any of the al-Murra strength, but he'd use Adnan's warrior skills. No way did he want the royal family to get wind of his presence in the kingdom. He'd keep this personal and close. Just him and the al-Murras—and maybe Grimaldi.

"Forget the Bolan name. You with me?"

"I am."

Bolan turned to the patriarch of the tribe. "You're Sunni." It was a statement.

The old man nodded.

"I have no proof yet, but I suspect a Shiite plot. Somehow they're a part of it. Maybe the Rashidis of Hail are being used as pawns. Your son might be called upon to kill many Shiites. Does that bother you?" he asked.

"He has killed for the British whenever they told him to kill. He has killed for pay. That sometimes bothered me. To kill a Shiite or many Shiites who are undermining our kingdom? It will bring honor to this house."

He turned and clapped his hands again. Servants came on the double. "A feast," he declared. "We will feast tonight and tomorrow you will be driven to Riyadh."

WHEN THE CAMP WAS ASLEEP, the patriarch left his wife's side and sat at the opening of his tent. The moon illuminated the rock outcroppings and massive dunes that stretched as far as the eye could see. The desert was his home. It always would be. The sprawling mass of sand was treacherous, would kill a man in hours if he didn't take precautions, but it was beautiful and gentle if a man loved it and made it his home.

When Allah decreed that the desert be wild and crazy, a man stayed with his family. He closed the flaps of his tent and folded the sides of his headdress around his mouth. It was a time to contemplate the power of the Almighty.

The night was also a time for thinking. The visitor was a man to contemplate. A few hours earlier he had entrusted his eldest son into the hands of this man. He knew that Adnan was capable, but the American was different. His heightened senses told him that this one was special, a man among men who attracted death and killing as food attracted flies. He would take the wrath of Allah with him into the camp of his enemies.

And the Rashidis were his enemies, men who professed to follow the five Pillars of Islam but who despoiled the earth and all around them.

The old man had ridden with Ibn Saud when he was younger. He had seen the blood vengeance of the Rashidi chiefs. Where Ibn Saud had killed ruthlessly in the name of Allah to further his cause, he was lenient with his captives, invited them to sit at his table, to join his family, to live out their lives in peace and love.

Not the Rashidis. Death was the only answer they had for long-term loyalty. Death was their panacea. If you were not a Rashidi or one of their closest tribal friends, your life was not worth the time it took to place your prayer rug and kneel.

He knew them. How well he knew them. The dregs of the earth, the curs of the kingdom, the last men on earth he would choose to call friend. Rule this kingdom? Rule justly with the billions of dollars at stake? He could not see it.

The Saudis had spent hundreds of billions on port facilities, on water, education, health and the necessary infrastructure to bring the kingdom into the twentieth century.

The Rashidis would invite in strangers to help them fight to gain their ends. They would distribute wealth among their cronies. Every decent Saudi would be stripped of what was rightfully his and would probably be left destitute or dead. The old man would send out all of his sons, all of his tribe, it if meant bringing this scourge under control.

The thoughts that plagued him churned in his gut. The acid that ate away at his ulcer brought pain. He reached in his robe for a couple of white disks and popped them into his mouth. He had thrust civilization from himself when younger and raised his family as peaceful Bedouin. But civilization was still a part of him. He had his water truck and his antacid pills. He had a son who had the fighting skills of a modern warrior.

The patriarch placed his life in the arms of Allah, on the talents of his eldest son and their new ally.

May their aim be true.

THE TWO MEN WERE DRIVEN to Riyadh in the Mercedes limousine. On the way Bolan told Adnan what had happened to date, including the fact he had money stashed away in the trunk of an old car. Al-Murra was obviously warming to the job. He had been trained as one of the finest fighting men in the world and had languished too long in the tent of his father in the desert. He was like a tiger on a short leash. All Bolan had to do was instruct him, point him in the right direction and give him the go-ahead.

In Riyadh Bolan took almost an hour to check out the hotel. His room at the El-Kureigi was still as safe as when he'd checked in. Al-Murra had taken a room for himself. They left wearing native costume. Al-Murra had suggested they comb the coffee houses and souks to find someone who knew where the Rashidis were holed up in Hail. It was a fair-sized city. Being chiefs of the local tribe, the Rashidis could easily have the local police in their pockets. It had probably been that way in the territory for centuries.

"How strong are they?" Bolan asked as they drove their rented car to the souks near the clock tower.

"Eight brothers are the nucleus now. They probably have five or six thousand followers in the area. The family name is Rashid. The tribe is Shammar, but everyone refers to them as the Rashidis."

"Could we have other tribes in one this?" Bolan asked.

"I doubt it. When Ibn Saud consolidated the whole peninsula, it took a long time, almost forty years. Arabia was ruled by tribal chiefs. They didn't give their loyalty to one man freely," al-Murra explained. "Ibn

Saud has been dead for more than thirty years. Our people still think of themselves as belonging to the old tribe, but their loyalty is to the royal family. The Rashidis are the only ones who are still militant.''

"So why don't the Saudis clean them out?"

"Because they're a peace-loving family. Ibn Saud granted immunity to all his old enemies and brought them into his family as one. They have built an air base at Hail, one of our biggest. The military police have a dual responsibility. They keep an eye on the Rashidis.''

Bolan didn't comment on the kind of job they were doing. If they were keeping an eye on the Rashidis, why had the rebellious tribe been able to knock off five Saudi princes?

Al-Murra had pulled into a huge parking lot to the east of the Friday Mosque. They walked through the souks, stopping to talk to merchants from time to time. After an hour with no success, they chose a rooftop teahouse to plan the rest of the evening.

"The man in the Western clothes two tables behind me," Bolan said. "You know who he is?"

"No."

"He's been following us for the past ten minutes. I recognize him from my stay at the central jail.''

"You were in one of our jails?"

"Yeah, but I broke out. The guy looks like CID.''

"We'd better go separate ways and meet back at the hotel," al-Murra suggested. "If he knows you and he's seen us together, we can't afford to let him tell anyone else.''

"My thinking exactly.''

"If he follows you, I'm going to keep on searching," al-Murra said. "See you later." He drank the rest of his tea and headed for the outside stairs and the street.

Bolan finished his tea slowly and left by another exit. The CID man followed him. When they got to the parking lot, Bolan started to enter the car next to the one they'd rented. The policeman poked a gun in through the window.

"Out," he commanded in English.

So he knew enough to use English, Bolan thought. Too bad. He didn't want to wage war on the police, but Jabbar had killed one of them already, and they probably blamed him equally. They were good, and they were persistent. He couldn't let this man report back that he'd seen the American with al-Murra. But he couldn't kill him, either.

He was tempted. Sedik was probably the kingpin of the baksheesh network, but that didn't make his men guilty.

"You one of Sedik's men?" he asked as he slid from the car.

"You have become an obsession with him, American. Twelve of Captain Sedik's best men had been assigned to you full-time. I will be honored for bringing you in."

"How did you recognize me?"

"A composite. Many people saw you at the punishments. You killed ten people."

Bad. Just what he'd been trying to avoid. Jabbar may have killed ten people, but the Sudanese was dead and Bolan had the label.

"You will keep your hands from yours sides and walk to my car," the CID man ordered. While they walked he asked, "Who was the man with you?"

"If you don't know, I'm not about to tell you."

"Captain Sedik has ways to make you talk. We'll see if you're so confident after an hour of persuasion."

Bolan had left his weapons at the hotel. He couldn't do anything but follow orders for now. When they reached an open space between the cars, he glanced around. They were alone and in an area not lighted by the few streetlights near the mosque.

He swung to the left and brought his right foot around in a powerful kick that caught the policeman in the ribs. The gun clattered to the ground, and the CID man collapsed to his knees.

Bolan moved forward to follow through, but the cop was quicker than the Executioner expected. He swung his good arm and caught Bolan in the groin, sending a wave of pain in all directions. He, too, went to his knees, gasping for air.

Eye to eye, the policeman grinned triumphantly through his pain. He was still the winner. He tried to stand and at the same time reach for the handcuffs clipped to his belt. He made the mistake of taking his eyes off Bolan. The warrior clasped both hands together and clubbed him behind the ear.

No one was around. With pain radiating from his groin, the soldier stood and dragged the cop to the rental. He found the keys under the front seat where al-Murra had left them and stuffed the unconscious man in the trunk.

All the way to the car dealer's, Bolan cursed his bad luck. The man had picked him out of a crowd. He couldn't have seen him more than once or twice at the jail. The *guttra* hid most of his face, so the composite they had must be very good.

When he rounded Al-Issam Road, which led to Khurais and Dammam, he remembered spotting a whole field of abandoned truck bodies. He headed for them and steered a path between the dust-covered hulks until he was hidden from the road.

One old metal box stood with its tires flat and its bed touching the ground. Bolan drove the rental into the truck bed slowly, shifting the weight to the front so that the wreck righted itself as it took the car's weight up front. The move freed up the rusted doors that had been stuck in the hardpan of the lot. The Executioner closed the doors, snapped the two pieces of the hasp together and stuck a rusty spike through the loop. The heat of the old cab would kill the CID man in hours and mummify the corpse in a day or two. The extreme heat would eliminate the usual smell of decomposition. No one would find him. Bolan sighed. He wouldn't let the man die.

The warrior walked to a dealer's lot and pounded on the door, waking up the salesman who had fallen asleep behind his desk. The young man hurried forward to unlock the door.

"What can I do for you?" he asked.

"I want a Suburban."

"I have a Nissan. Much better. Four-wheel-drive, tape deck, many extras the Suburban doesn't have."

Bolan wasn't in the mood to argue. He paid the man with the rest of the cash he had on him, signed the papers and was on his way in minutes. He had one stop to make before going back to the hotel. The Chrysler. It was time to make another withdrawal.

He pulled over to a pay phone on Airport Road, called the police and told them where to find their man. The poor bastard had only been doing his job, and Bolan couldn't kill a cop.

But what about the rogue cop himself? If Bolan had the hammer down on Sedik, would he pull the trigger? Would he have left Sedik to mummify in the truck?

Bolan just didn't know the answer, and he hoped he'd never be faced with the decision.

8

"We will be naming a new king soon," al-Murra said to Bolan. "The pilgrimage is only days away. I agree with you that the action is tied in with the pilgrimage somehow."

"You learn anything more at the souks?"

"Rumors. I suspect some come close to the truth."

"Such as? Tell me more about the pilgrimage," Bolan asked.

"First, everyone is expecting the selection of a stronger king. You understand the process?"

"I've been briefed on it."

"When the king is appointed, we usually celebrate, but the timing is all wrong. The first of the king's duties will be to humble himself at the pilgrimage, to lead the worshipers in obeisance to Allah."

"Tell me first how the pilgrimage starts."

Al-Murra drained the small mug of tea and thought through the process for a few seconds. "Muslims come from all over the world," he finally said. "They used to come by land, some came by sea. Most of them come by air now. Jidda is the usual port of entry."

"Yes, but what do they do first?"

"The ones who are not hajjis—who haven't been on pilgrimage before—take off to the north for the city of

Medina. The tomb of Mohammed is located there beneath the Mosque of the Green Dome."

"Does the king go there?"

"No. Not everyone makes the minor pilgrimage."

"Then we rule that out. When does the new king make his first appearance?"

"On the first day. It is the ruler's duty to wash the floor of the holy Kabah on his hands and knees."

"Who's at the ceremony?" Bolan asked, feeling a sense of foreboding creeping up his spine like a chill.

"It's public. Millions of pilgrims are inside the mosque. They're all trying to get as close to the ceremony as possible. It's a madness that possesses them, a religious fervor. I've felt it."

"We've got to stop that ceremony."

"You can't stop it," al-Murra said. "It must go on."

"I've got a bad feeling about this. The ceremony would be the perfect place to take out the king. They could hold millions captive, but what would that accomplish?"

"They'd probably declare the coming of a new prophet. Have a phony prophet on hand to talk to the people. Convert them to new Muslim leadership in the holiest place on earth," al-Murra said. "Muslims can be just as gullible as Christians, and they'd be in the mood, in the very center of their religious world."

The Executioner took a few seconds trying to think it through. "Is there any way to exclude Shiites from the pilgrimage?"

"No."

"Then it's a powder keg. Could be an all-out war that could make the 1979 rebellion at the Great Mosque look like a tea party."

Al-Murra sat with his chin in his hands. "This is all supposition so far. You could be right, but first we have to know for sure. What's the next move?"

"How much time do we have?" Bolan asked.

"Eight days to the ceremony."

"All right. Take the Nissan and head for Hail. Locate the Rashidi safehouse and find out all you can," Bolan commanded. "I'm going to call my home base for help." He told the Bedouin about Jack Grimaldi and the hidden Cessna. "We'll fly into Hail as pesticide experts in a couple of days. We'll pick a teahouse next to the biggest hotel for our next meet. Look for us."

MURID AZZIZ MURSHED lay on a hospital bed with an intravenous tube feeding fluids into him at maximum rate. He was pale. A doctor hovered over him, giving orders for continued care to a nurse standing by.

Captain Sedik paced near the foot of the bed. Lieutenant Bindagii stood by the door. The doctor had ordered them out, but Sedik's response had been no more than a grunt and a harsh look. Sedik and Bindagii had rushed to the truck graveyard, hoping to find their man lucid and able to give them immediate information, but he was unconscious and unable to talk. Now he was conscious, but his throat was still constricted.

"I must talk to him immediately," Sedik said, breaking the silence.

"He cannot talk. I want him to rest," the doctor answered.

"He can rest later. Can he understand?" the captain asked.

"Yes."

"Then get out of my way." Sedik pushed the doctor aside. "Murid," he said gently, "if you hear me well, nod your head."

The man, his face the color of the hospital sheets, nodded weakly.

"Was it the American?"

A nod.

"Was he tall with dark hair as I described him to you?"

Another nod.

"Do you know where he was going?"

The dehydrated man shook his head.

"Was he armed? Did he have an opportunity to kill you earlier?"

A nod.

"What are you getting at?" Bindagii asked.

"The American called in to tell us where Murid was," Sedik said impatiently. "He could have killed him at any time. Doesn't that tell you something?"

"But he killed our man at the pesticide camp."

"I'm not so sure," the captain replied. "He had an accomplice. The man who was shot in Abu Dhabi. I have reports our American didn't do any of the killing at the execution site, and yet he killed in Abu Dhabi. Something strange about this one."

He turned back to the sick officer and found that he was asleep.

The doctor reached over and felt for a pulse, nodding in satisfaction. "He's exhausted," he said to the CID men. "I'd advise you to wait a few hours. He'll regain his speech and be stronger."

"Come on, Bindagii," Sedik said. "We'll come back later."

"What do you plan to do next?" Bindagii asked.

"You and I follow up any incident in the kingdom involving a tall American."

"The foreigners all look alike to me."

"True. We might have some false leads, but we have to follow them all."

"We can't cover the whole kingdom."

"We'll have a helicopter standing by. I'll call the minister as soon as we get back to the office."

Bindagii thought about the plan while they walked to their staff car. "Do you think he's responsible for the killings?" he asked.

"Frankly, no," Sedik said, lengthening his stride as they left the hospital. "But I'd sure like to know what's so important to him that he's willing to face the sword."

"He seems to have unlimited funds. Who do you think is behind him?" Bindagii asked as if to himself.

Sedik didn't answer. He had several theories but none seemed to fit. Someone had to be backing the American. Normally he'd be sure it was the CIA, but they didn't have the scruples this man had. Parts of the puzzle just didn't fit. But that was all right with him. The puzzle always intrigued. He'd have the answers before he was finished. This was his private preserve and all exits had been closed. It was just a matter of the spider finding the spot in his web where the poor fly had been trapped.

"So AL-MURRA IS my intelligence man. We're hooking up in a few days," Bolan said to Brognola, concluding his update. He could picture the man from Justice chewing on a cigar and fidgeting in his chair. He would run a hand through his hair. His tie would be askew and he'd look worried.

"What can I do at this end?"

"Where's Jack Grimaldi?"

"Honduras. He's just finished a job with Phoenix Force."

"I need him," Bolan said. "I need a crack pilot. We'll be doing some low-level stuff here, and I've got an idea or two about an escape plan."

"How long to wrap it up?" Brognola asked.

"I see us making it out of here in just over a week."

"Watch yourself, Striker. Seems you've got enemies on every side."

"Can't be helped. Just get Grimaldi over here tomorrow night at the latest. Fly him to one of the carriers in the Gulf, then bring him in under radar to the place northeast of Majma'a where you dropped the cash. I've still got the Cessna there. I'll have the running lights on. He should be able to spot them."

"What's he supposed to do? Sprout wings?"

"He's an expert in free-fall. Anyway, that's his problem. And, Hal, have the chopper drop off some goodies, okay? Three SMGs and a dozen clips. A small case of grenades. Some black fatigues."

"Okay. It'll be tight, but he should be there by midnight tomorrow."

THE DRIVE FROM RIYADH to Hail took al-Murra longer than he figured. The Nissan gave him trouble. A split hose in the coolant system delayed him in Buraida for hours. He thought about the strange American and what he would be doing. If he didn't move faster, Bolan would be in Hail with his friend before he could get there himself.

The city just south of An-Nafud was bustling with trade when he pulled in, exhausted. Two Toyota pickups, each with two young camels in the back, passed him on the road in. His people hadn't used camels as transport for years. Small Japanese pickups had replaced them. In his tribe they were experimenting with camels as sources of milk. With selective breeding and artificial insemination, they had already increased the yield by three hundred percent. When you lived three hundred miles from the nearest town, you had to be self-sufficient.

His father had been wise. One of Adnan's brothers had been sent to Japan to become a motor mechanic. Another had been apprenticed as a plumber, another as a carpenter. It might not have been apparent to Bolan during his visit, but the desert wanderers weren't wanderers anymore.

Hail was different than most Saudi cities, perhaps because the Rashidis had so much influence there. The veiling of women was more severe; smoking was frowned on; all the men carried arms. It was as far from Riyadh in everyday habits as was possible.

Al-Murra sought out the biggest hotel, the Intercontinental, and parked near the closest teahouse. This was where he would meet Bolan and his friend.

"God's peace be with you," he said to the bowing proprietor.

"And with you," came the traditional response.

"I will have tea," al-Murra declared. "And if you have a chicken? Perhaps some rice?"

"The best in Hail," the grinning proprietor replied.

Al-Murra sat back to watch the passing crowd. The room had only a dozen tables and most were filled. A young man sauntered to the table and sat across from him without asking, as was the custom.

"May God go with you," the young man said.

"And with you," al-Murra responded.

"You are not from here," the youth observed.

Al-Murra realized he was wearing a *guttra* of black-and-white checks while all the natives were wearing their winter red-and-white checked headdresses.

"My home is near Al-Ubayla in the Rub' al-Khali," al-Murra replied truthfully.

"You are lucky," the youth said, his mouth turning down at the corners. "A true Bedouin. My people were Bedouin but settled here. I hate it here."

"Are you not being rash to speak so?" al-Murra asked, taking the tea the proprietor had brought and sipping the hot liquid carefully.

"This town is a fortress. If you are not Rashidi, you are nothing."

"And you are not a Rashidi?"

"Never. I know what they are. Shiite fanatics," the youth spit.

"Watch your tongue," al-Murra warned. "You could end up in big trouble."

"The stranger is right, Sultan. You never know who is listening," the proprietor said as he placed a platter in front of al-Murra.

"You, too?" Al-Murra was surprised. "You sound like our young friend. Doesn't anyone here like the Rashidis?"

"Those who bow and scrape. The bullies and the thieves. They all support the Rashidis," the older man said with venom.

"I caution you to hold your tongue," al-Murra repeated. "Talking against them in public can only give you trouble." He speared the chicken with a knife held in his left hand and pulled off a leg with his right. As he began to eat, he looked them both in the eye. "Action is better than words. But be careful you don't get caught." He winked as he continued to eat.

The proprietor moved off to serve someone else. The youth pulled himself to his feet, threw the ends of his *guttra* across each shoulder and took off down the dusty street.

A man in native clothes drank the rest of his tea, put some money on the table and followed the young man.

THE MOON SHONE BRIGHTLY between the towering buttes where Bolan waited. Occasionally a cloud would hide the moon and the area would blacken.

Bolan had described the place to Brognola carefully, and the coordinates were the same as last time. He had expected Grimaldi at least two hours ago. Perhaps they had run into trouble.

His ears were tuned for rotor blades when he caught the faintest hint of engine noise at about two thousand feet. He ran to the Cessna and turned on the port and starboard running lights. Within minutes he heard the wind change above his head, saw the moon hidden momentarily by a canopy of cloth and heard the crunch of paratrooper boots on the hardpan.

The Executioner unleathered his gun and cautiously approached the figure now busy unstrapping the harness of his rig. Bolan holstered the Beretta when he could finally make out Grimaldi's features in the moonlight.

"Am I glad to see you!" the warrior greeted the veteran pilot. The two men had been through a lot together, had fought many battles. He'd always been able to rely on Jack Grimaldi. The guy was as much of a soldier as any he'd served with when the chips were down.

They didn't have time for catching up before two bundles sailed to the ground beside them.

"Looks like you made it without detection," Bolan said. "If they'd picked you up on radar or AWACS they'd be on us by now. Let's get these things unpacked before we get caught up on the news."

Brognola had come through with everything Bolan had ordered, but sent nothing that would indicate the presence of an American operative. The SMGs were Ultimax 100s manufactured by CIS of Singapore, each with three extra clips of a hundred rounds. The grenades were Chinese, fifty phosphorus and fifty fragmentation. The load included Swedish survival knives, black fatigues, combat cosmetics, SIG-Sauer 9 mm automatics, two AN/AVP night vision sights and one distant sound detector. A small leather case contained three kinds of drugs complete with syringes. Bolan knew he wouldn't use the drugs, but he wasn't about to throw them away.

"Let's get all this stuff to the plane," Bolan suggested. "It's good to see your ugly face," he added.

"I don't know what you've got yourself into, but I was getting bored. Once you've seen one Sandinista you've seen them all. I like the crate," Grimaldi continued, nodding toward the light plane. "First time I've seen an almost-new Cessna. You bring it in?"

"Partly. I had a Sudanese CIA field man who helped. He's dead."

"Like that, is it?"

"All the way. We've got someone else working with us. He's in Hail waiting for us. A Saudi who trained with Beckwith at an SAS camp."

"Red Garrett told me about a guy from Saudi who trained with him at the SAS school way back. The Arab was just a kid at the time, but one hell of a soldier."

"Adnan al-Murra. How would Garrett know him?"

"Being a broker, Red makes it a point to know everything about every man who's worth anything in a fight," Grimaldi informed him, lighting a cigarette as he helped load their equipment onto the plane.

"You smoking around planes these days?" Bolan asked.

Grimaldi squashed the smoke under foot. "You get careless in Honduras. Bored."

"Just don't get bored enough to be careless here, okay?"

"You got it."

"Al-Murra's in Hail doing legwork." Bolan went on to explain about the Saudi deaths and the Rashidi connection as he knew it. He also mentioned his being in trouble with the CID.

"So what else is new? But it's okay now, soldier. Grimaldi's here. We're getting this thing in gear. The Rashidis don't have a chance."

AL-MURRA WAS about to leave the teahouse when the proprietor sat down at the table, filling the chair to overflowing.

"What was all the talk about Rashidis with the young one?" he asked.

Al-Murra was on guard immediately. When the man had joined the discussion earlier, he'd seemed ill-disposed to the family that ran the town. "Just talk," he replied. "Nothing more than that."

The proprietor leaned toward him conspiratorially. "When the young one left, someone followed him. They might have an eye on you. Be careful."

"What is this, a police town? Aren't you afraid of talking to me?"

"You're right. It's a town in the pocket of the Rashidis. And, no, I'm not afraid of them," the older man said defiantly. "I'm a known quantity. They know I'm harmless."

"You'd better be careful yourself, old man," al-Murra advised.

"Allah curse them and all their family."

"Where are their headquarters?" the Bedouin asked casually.

The proprietor stopped to snap at a lazy waiter who was letting customers stack up. "Umm al-Qulban is their real home base. It is like a fortress. Their headquarters here is just a large compound. It's well guarded, but not like their home up north."

"How far north?"

The old man leaned closer. "Only one road leads north from here. After twenty miles, at Al-Wuqid, it branches right and left. Umm al-Qulban is to the left about thirty miles farther."

"You are a true man of the one God," al-Murra told him, smiling. "You can do two other things for me."

"Anything to help one who hates the Rashidis as much as I."

"Where is their headquarters here?"

"I'd stay away from it, friend."

Al-Murra gripped the older man by the shoulder and squeezed reassuringly. "I can take care of myself, old friend. Tell me where they are."

"The last compound north on King Faisal Street. What are you going to do?"

"It's better that you don't know."

"What is the other thing you wanted to know?"

"Not something I have to know. I want to leave a message for some friends who will come looking for me."

"I'll leave some paper and pen in the toilet room at the end of the hall." The old man pointed to a scarred door to the right. "Leave the note. I will pick it up. I don't want anyone to see you writing at the table."

"You are a man among men. Be assured our work is for the house of Saud."

"I care not who you work for, only those you work against." The old man grinned, the stumps of the teeth in his lower jaw showing as his grin widened. "How will I know your friends?" he asked as he stood to get the notepaper.

"Two Americans. I don't know what they will be wearing, but probably Western clothes. We were to meet here, but I might be busy."

The proprietor disappeared through the scarred door, al-Murra following a few minutes later. He had checked the crowd at the teahouse and those loitering around the immediate area. He saw no one suspicious. He walked to the toilet room and saw a small notepad and a pencil near the hole on the floor.

He stood and wrote in English, an act he hadn't performed for some time. The writing came out as a scrawl, but readable.

Hail base is the last compound at the north end of King Faisal Street. Stronghold at Umm al-Qulban north of here. I'm taking a look. Al-M.

The proprietor watched as the Bedouin walked away and went to retrieve the note. He read the English with great difficulty, but his three years of indifferent study at the secondary school many years ago was enough.

He had a feeling about the man who had just left. He hadn't always been a teahouse owner. In his youth he had seen much. He had defied his family and fought with the Jordanese in the 1967 war, and he knew the look of a warrior. The stranger who had just left had that look.

Maybe it would happen after all. Maybe the Rashidis would finally meet someone who could deal them a killing blow.

He had prayed for the day. Now he had to control his impatience, his curiosity and his tongue until the note was picked up.

He wasn't sure he could manage it, but he would try.

9

At first light Grimaldi opened his eyes and reached for his cigarettes. The first Bolan was aware of the new day was the smell of cigarette smoke filling the cockpit. He didn't have to open his eyes to know the flier was ready for the day.

"You hungry?" he asked, opening his eyes. He stretched as much as the cockpit would allow, trying to give some relief to muscles that were cramped from the confined space he'd slept in.

After a full breakfast of ham and eggs—courtesy of Brognola's good thinking—Grimaldi checked the plane thoroughly, started her up and revved to listen to the engine.

"She's as sweet as a nut," he announced. "Where are we heading first?"

Bolan produced a rudimentary map and wished he'd asked Brognola for better ones. "Hail is here—" he pointed to a dot on the map north of a larger town called Buraida "—right on the edge of An-Nafud, the Red Desert."

"That's just great," Grimaldi complained. "We're right in the middle of the Gulf War, the AWACS planes are up and manned by our own guys and you want me to fly you three or four hundred miles across the heartland of the kingdom."

"Piece of cake. Just keep it low, that's all."

"These Saudis, the ones we're working for who don't know we're working for them, have F-16s. And they have the best radar in the world. It's all American-made. This is the worst place in the world to try to fly around undetected."

"That's why I chose you, pal," Bolan said. "You said Central America was boring. So let's get it on, okay?"

"Okay. Here's how we're going to do it. Look at the map," Grimaldi said. "Behind us about ten miles is a desert."

"Ad-Dahnah."

"Whatever. You notice it becomes the Red Desert up at the north end? So we fly over desert all the way and come in the back door."

"We got enough gas for that?"

"I don't know. It might be close. We should be all right," he said, pushing her to full revs and taking off into the wind.

He described a lazy turn to starboard, keeping the wing tip never more than a hundred feet off the sand. An hour later they saw smoke to the east.

"Only town on the map near here is Al-Shumul. Could be that," Bolan suggested.

"Might be oil burn-off. You know, from the wells?"

"Too far north. Isn't it about time we headed west?"

"Who's flying this crate? Give it another ten minutes. I got it figured."

In less than ten minutes they started to bank to port, heading due west. They followed a strip of asphalt that looked so black it had to be new that year.

"Five towns since we left the desert. They're on the map, but I can't pronounce them. Hail's got to be close. Maybe five miles south."

Grimaldi banked to the left, now only a few feet from the undulating hardpan. They both concentrated on the bleak landscape ahead. The ground started to form a series of large hills, rocky, hundreds of feet high. Scores of arroyos carved deep channels in the rock, some flat and at least two miles long.

"Keep below the level of the hills," Bolan directed. "They've got a major air base on the other side. F-16s."

"You kidding me?"

Grimaldi flew a few feet higher, spotted the air base on the other side of the hills and dipped below the crest, keeping his distance. "It'll be a miracle if they don't spot us."

"Just keep out of sight. Their radar can't work through rock."

"What makes you think they don't have some on the crest of the hills?"

"I've been scanning the hills, and I didn't see any."

"Lots of places to hide the crate," Grimaldi suggested.

"Maybe, but we'll have a long walk to town, and we'll have a hard time finding the plane when we come back—like coming home to a subdivision with a thousand houses all the same."

They flew on until the shape of the settlement stretched before them.

"Fly to a flat spot just north of town," Bolan suggested. "We're supposed to be legitimate insecticide specialists."

"I hope your papers are better than mine," Grimaldi said.

"What did he give you?"

"Nothing. I never saw him. Just a series of fast planes and one lousy parachute." Grimaldi focused his attention on bringing the airplane into the wind for a long approach north of town.

When the craft stopped rolling, Bolan hopped out and looked around. "Take her a few hundred yards into that small arroyo, out of the wind. Maybe get some shade," he suggested.

Grimaldi left him standing there, his back to the town. Just as Grimaldi reached the inner part of a slit in the rock, a black Mercedes came out of nowhere, heading straight for Bolan.

The Executioner wasn't waiting for introductions. He dived for cover behind a group of boulders, unleathered the Beretta and kept an eye on the dark car.

The Mercedes stopped a hundred feet from him. Two men jumped out and took cover. Their appearance triggered something in Bolan's mind.

The Soviet Union. He'd seen the type in Moscow. Even at a hundred feet they were unmistakable.

Where had they come from? They must have been touring the city, or patrolling. But why? Did the Rashidis have connections with the Soviets? This whole thing was getting complicated.

He'd been thinking about the men and not concentrating on what they were doing. One had run around a series of rocks and flanked him on the left while his companion stayed near the car.

Bolan concentrated on the man to the left. The warrior glanced quickly at the plane. The prop was still turning, and Grimaldi was still inside.

The man to his left popped up from behind a rock and fired. Chips of granite showered around Bolan, cutting into his arm and nicking his cheek.

Out of the corner of his eye he saw movement again to his left. The open man was slipping from boulder to boulder. Bolan waited for the guy's next move and fired a 3-round burst, scoring. The man crouching behind the car hadn't moved. Bolan could still see his shadow.

The Executioner crept from rock to rock. He wasn't worried about the man at the car. The range was too far. What the hell kind of strategy was this for a couple of pros? It seemed like a no-win situation for them.

As Bolan neared the vehicle, the second man leaped inside the passenger door and, scrambled across the seat into the driver's seat. He gunned the engine in his haste to get out of there, and the vehicle sped away, spewing gravel in its wake.

Nothing made sense. The whole scene had been a stupid play. They must have thought they had a couple of amateurs at their mercy.

He approached the dead man with caution. He kicked away the gun, an old Soviet TT-33 Tokarev. Most Soviet agents used the heavier Makarov now, but a few still stuck with the smaller weapon.

The man was undoubtedly Soviet or was at least posing as one. The suit was so bad it could have only been made behind the iron curtain. The rigid facial features were Slavic. Bolan went through the man's pockets but found nothing.

"What do you think?" Grimaldi said, standing behind him, an Ultimax 100 at the ready, pointed at the sky.

"Don't know. We're supposed to think they're Soviet or that they were and underestimated us."

"Makes sense," Grimaldi said. "If your suspicions are right, why wouldn't the Soviets get in on the act? If the ayatollahs are into this, and it'll shake up the Gulf, who will gain the most?"

"It sounds right, but I can't see them in bed with the Shiites. Last I heard the Soviets were going to send troops in to help the Iraqis." Bolan shook his head, frustrated. "Put the Ultimax away and get yourself a SIG-Sauer. Let's go into town and see what al-Murra has dug up for us."

AT THE COMPOUND four of the brothers saw the Mercedes return with only one Soviet. Hamza walked to the vehicle as it came to a stop.

"What happened?"

"We were on a routine patrol," the Soviet said, his English almost impossible to follow. "A small aircraft landed north of here. Two men, maybe American, fired on us. Alexei was killed."

"You can take us to them?"

"It was one of the cracks in the hills. So many of them. I left in a hurry...."

"Useless." Hamza cursed in Arabic, turning to his brothers. "So the one who killed our cousin in Abu Dhabi has survived the Rub' al-Khali. He has another with him. What do you think?" he asked as they walked to his house.

"He will come here," an older brother offered. "Why else would he be here?"

"Good. I agree," Hamza said. "We don't have to do anything special. We prepare for him here."

"What does he want?" another brother asked, a man who had suffered the cruelties of desert living. He was almost blind from a parasitic disease common to the area. One of his sons guided him most of the time.

"A good question," Hamza replied, stroking his small chin beard. "He is obviously here to stop us. Perhaps Abdul Rachman did tell him what he knew before he died. We have to assume he knows we are behind the Saudi deaths. But does he know what we plan? I don't think so. If we take him now, it will be over," he concluded as he led them into their midday meal.

He thought about the American as he walked across the tiled open area of the compound. Maybe he'd better play it safe and lay a trap outside the compound. No need for the others to know. He would talk to the Soviet after their meal.

BOLAN TOOK A BEARING from a pocket compass and reversed the reading to give him the general heading back to the plane. He made a mental note that the Cessna would need gas.

"How do we get to town?" Grimaldi asked.

"We hike it. Follow the tire tracks of the Mercedes."

"Walking's not my strong suit," Grimaldi grumbled. "That's why I took up flying."

They followed the tracks for a couple of miles until the sun's heat chased them to the shade of a series of hills that led them closer to town.

"Remind me to steal a car to make it back," Grimaldi said, mopping sweat from his chin.

On the outskirts of town people were performing their usual midafternoon tasks. They all stopped to stare at the strangers—Westerners were uncommon in the northern community.

"Let's get out of sight," Bolan said as he waved at a small yellow cab.

"Take us to the biggest hotel," he commanded the driver.

The man muttered something in Arabic and drove to a marketplace in the next block. He waved over a merchant and spoke to him.

"The driver doesn't understand you," the man said, leaning in the window, his face wrinkled by years of desert sun.

"We want the biggest hotel in town," Grimaldi repeated.

"That will be the Intercontinental," the merchant replied, withdrawing from the window. He spoke to the taxi driver and waved as they drove off in a cloud of dust.

The streets were paved in the center of town. Obviously some planning had been done. The Intercontinental was on one side of a spacious square. The rest of the buildings were large and impressive, obviously new. Around the corner from the hotel a teahouse spilled into the street.

Bolan and Grimaldi climbed out of the cab.

"Two hundred," the Bedouin cabbie demanded in the only English he knew.

"Two hundred!" Grimaldi started to argue.

Bolan squeezed his shoulder. He paid the cabbie the two hundred riyals, almost seventy dollars, and headed for the teahouse. "Don't make waves," he warned. "We don't want to draw attention to ourselves."

A huge man greeted them as they sank into chairs wearily.

"You are welcome in my establishment," he said, towering over them.

"Tea," Bolan said. "And a chicken with rice," he added.

"I'm not crazy about chicken and rice, Mack."

"You wouldn't like the alternatives," Bolan said. "We'll see what the hotel has if we check in later."

The big man appeared, bearing two steaming plates, each piled high with white rice and topped with a full roasted chicken. He put one sharp knife at each plate. "We don't see many strangers here," he said as he took the mugs of tea from his tray. "Just yesterday a man from the south ordered chicken and rice. A man much like yourself," he went on, nodding at Bolan. "He was a Bedouin from the Rub' al-Khali. Looked like he might have been a military man."

The proprietor left them to their meal and their thoughts.

"What was all that about?" Grimaldi asked as he tore a leg off the steaming chicken.

"He just described al-Murra. Our SAS friend must have left word here. The big guy is just testing."

"So?"

"So we eat and talk later."

The other customers glared as Grimaldi went at the chicken with both hands and shoveled up the rice on the blade of the knife. A waiter refilled their tea mugs constantly. The proprietor hovered in the background, looking up and down the street carefully and scrutinizing his patrons with care. When he came to clear the empty plates, he placed the note discreetly near Bolan's hand.

The warrior pocketed the note and led the way to the hotel.

"We going to check in here?" Grimaldi asked.

"I've changed my mind. You have no papers, and in a place like this they'd want to see your passport. We'll use a Bedouin hotel. We might not have time to sleep."

"What's a Bedouin hotel?" Grimaldi asked.

"You'll see soon enough," Bolan said, sinking into a chair in the lobby. He unfolded the note and read al-Murra's scrawl.

"Al-Murra knows where the two Rashidi strongholds are and he's gone to the first one by himself," Bolan whispered to Grimaldi.

"When?"

"Must have been yesterday, after he wrote this."

"What do you figure?"

The Executioner scowled over the paper. "This note was insurance. He should have been here to meet us. They've got him."

"So they know we're coming."

"I don't think al-Murra would give up information willingly. We still might have a chance."

"So what's our plan?" Grimaldi asked.

"Find transport and go back to the plane," Bolan said. "Full battle gear. Come back after dark and pull out our buddy."

"Now we're cooking! How do we classify these guys? Do we go in smoking?"

"Everyone in the compound is an enemy. We take prisoners if any of the brothers are still there."

They left the hotel on foot. Grimaldi followed Bolan to the parking lot behind the hotel, where at least a hundred cars were parked unattended. It was late afternoon, and the shadow cast by the hotel gave them moderate cover as they walked among the cars making their choice.

Some vehicles had been sitting there a long time and were covered in dust. Bolan chose a Toyota, jimmied the lock and hot-wired the ignition. They headed out of the lot in seconds with the wipers turned on to clear away some of the grit.

Bolan headed north. Traffic was light, and many of the vehicles were as dusty as theirs, which meant no one paid special attention to them.

Before leaving town, Bolan found King Faisal Street and headed toward the hills that towered over the town like avenging angels in the fading light. The last compound on the right stood by itself. It was huge. The concrete block and stucco wall surrounding it was at least twelve feet high. The steel gates at the front stood open, guarded on each side by a man with a submachine gun slung over his shoulder.

In the few seconds it took to drive past the open gates, Bolan saw at least a half-dozen houses in the compound—probably one for each brother—and one large building that stood in the middle of the compound, probably a meeting house. Where would they keep al-Murra? The soldier knew he needed more information.

By the time they cleared the last street it was starting to get dark. Night fell like a blanket at this latitude. Getting back to the plane might be more difficult than anticipated.

10

As Bolan was about to step from the truck, he saw something at the edge of his vision, barely visible in the area covered by the headlights.

"Hit the dirt!" he yelled.

He dropped to the ground and rolled under the truck as a swarm of slugs churned up dirt around him.

"You okay, Jack?"

"Yeah. No sweat," the pilot called back. "I'm heading for the rocks on my side. This whole thing could blow."

"I'll take them from the left." Bolan turned to snake his way to a cluster of rocks on his side.

It was quiet. The truck lights shone on the Cessna, and he could see the other object, a stake truck parked off to one side. The enemy was hidden in clusters of rocks on either side of the Cessna.

Rifle fire tore at the Toyota. Fingers of steel moved along her sides, reaching out for the gas tank. The explosion sent out a wave of concussion and lit up the night sky.

Bolan could see the tops of several heads behind the rocks. Red-and-white-checked *guttras* were caught in the fierce light of the fire, but they were out of range. He would have to go in and get them.

The fire started to wane. Bolan turned his back, shut his eyes and remained out of sight for a full two minutes. Then, with his back to the fire, he slipped from rock to rock, circling around his enemy.

They were still looking toward the fire. He kept his eyes away from the dull glow to retain the degree of night vision he'd gained. They didn't hear him. He could see the back of a half-dozen Rashidi warriors from his new perch. Was that all of them?

Where was Grimaldi? Bolan had to assume his buddy had worked with him often enough that he'd figure out the play.

Each Rashidi had a Kalashnikov aimed at the truck— Bolan could see the AKs' distinctive orange-colored banana clips. He could get maybe three of them before they'd have time to zero in on him. If Grimaldi hadn't made it to the rocks, he'd take at least two, maybe three, and duck back to take up a new position.

Bolan knelt behind a rock, steadied his gun hand on the smooth surface, clasped his wrist for support and zeroed in on the head of the nearest man. He squeezed off a shot, then swung his weapon to the next target and the next. Each shot was a winner, but each seemed to have an echo. The targets went down one at a time, but others went down as if a giant mirror had been positioned to his left, showing a simultaneous repetition of the scene. He realized it was the result of Grimaldi's SIG-Sauer barking out its wrath. They took out six Rashidis in no more than ten seconds.

The gunfire died down. The glow of red-hot metal remained, along with a flicker of flame from the spare tire at the back of the wreck. The smell of burning rubber attacked his nostrils.

It was quiet and it was dark. Bolan decided to wait them out. He had time to wait, and he assumed Grimaldi would do the same.

Twenty minutes passed. Nothing moved. It was time to count the dead. Bolan moved like a mountain cat from rock to rock. He knew exactly where each man had gone down.

The first man lay on one side, half his head blown away, the rock crimson behind him. Bolan crept to the next and the next. They were motionless.

"Jack," he called from behind cover.

"Over here," the shout came back.

"I count three on this side. Are we clear?"

"I have three. One is still breathing. I'm taking him down to their truck."

They had only the light of the moon from behind the towering hills. The Rashidi truck was army surplus, an old stake job they'd obviously used for garbage detail. It still stank.

Grimaldi came out of darkness, carrying a body over his shoulder. He eased the wounded Rashidi down beside the vehicle and grinned at his partner. "One more win for our side." He seemed more cheerful, his old self, as if a weight had been lifted from his shoulders.

"No time to gloat," Bolan said. "Plenty more where they came from. We still don't know where the final battle's going to be." He waved his Beretta at the Rashidi while he spoke, then holstered it. "Can this one talk?" he asked.

They pulled him into a brighter patch of light. His face was pale, and a chest wound bled into his robe. Bolan turned him over. Several holes oozed blood.

"He's not going to talk. Let's look over the truck," Bolan suggested.

All the supplies that Brognola had sent were piled in the back of the truck. The big surprise was three steel drums of aviation fuel.

"What's this?" Bolan asked, holding up a bunch of wires.

"Smarter than I thought," Grimaldi said. "It's part of the plane's electrical system."

"Can you put it back?"

"No sweat. Take about a half hour. But why bring fuel and then disable the plane?"

"Don't ask me to explain how they think," Bolan said. "Who knows?"

"What now?" Grimaldi asked.

"We've got all night. You fix the electrical system, I fuel the plane, then we move it to a safe place and head for town. I still want to know what the final play's going to be," the Executioner said. "Maybe someone at the Hail compound can tell us."

IT WAS QUIET in Hail. Unlike Riyadh, no youths swarmed the streets or sat watching TV in groups around their cars. Air force ground patrols were out. The two Americans managed to avoid them. They had cleaned up two Rashidi robes and headdresses and pulled them on over their fighting gear.

Local police were out in full force, but the soldiers made it to the compound without incident. They left the truck in the shadow of a house under construction and pulled off the Rashidi clothing.

They looked like two visions from the depths of hell. The warriors were in black fatigues, stevedore caps, black combat cosmetics and black sneakers. Their webbing held an assortment of hardware hung like tree ornaments at Christmas. Each had an Ultimax 100 slung over his shoulder and extra clips on the webbing.

Nothing stirred in the compound. "What do you think?" Grimaldi asked as he huddled at the foot of the towering wall.

"Maybe they think we're dead. Had to think that six men in ambush would be enough, right?"

"Do you really think so?"

"No, I think they're smarter than we give them credit for. I don't pretend to understand why they think the way they do, but I never said they were stupid. Let's get with it. Only one way to find out what we want."

Grimaldi put his back to the wall and hoisted Bolan up. The soldier scanned the compound for the enemy and reached down for the extended arm. From their perch they stretched out on their bellies, head to head, and surveyed the grounds. On a signal from Bolan they dropped to the tiled inner court of the compound and snaked along the wall, looking over the security.

Two guards lounged at the front gate. The black figures kept to the shadow of the wall and crept closer. Bolan waved at Grimaldi, then launched himself across the open space at the guard on the other side while Grimaldi took the near one. They used a classic attack without giving it a second thought, one arm around the throat, knee in the back, commando knife slashed across the throat.

Bolan nodded to Grimaldi and hoisted his man to hang him on a piece of the filigreed steel door. He looked like he was leaning lazily at his post.

Grimaldi followed suit and trailed Bolan across the compound to the back gate, which was locked. Only one guard was evident, on a prayer mat with his back to the wall.

Bolan pulled the Beretta and threaded on the customized silencer. He aimed with care and put a bullet through the man's temple at twenty yards.

They had made no noise. The guards were still at their posts. It was time to tackle the houses.

"We have to take the next one we see alive," Bolan whispered to his friend. "We don't know where they have al-Murra."

Grimaldi nodded and pointed to the first house.

Bolan went in the front door quickly and dived to one side, surprising a servant carrying an empty tray. Startled, the man turned, and dropped the tray. Bolan caught it, eased it to the floor and took the man by the throat in one fluid motion. When Grimaldi came through the door, Bolan cocked his head toward an inner door.

The room was furnished in the manner of a Western living room, and looked as if it were seldomly used. Bolan kept his hand over the servant's mouth while he pulled him over to a settee.

"Give me the drug case," he whispered to Grimaldi. He had no intention of using the drugs, but knew the vials could be useful props in the drama to come.

The pilot handed over the case. Bolan eased his hand off the servant's mouth. "If you cry out, I'll kill you," he said, not knowing whether the man could speak English or not.

The man nodded.

"This is a powerful drug," Bolan continued, showing the man one of the vials. "I need some information. Give it to me now, or I'll use the drug." He hoped the bluff would save him some time.

"Please, English," the man choked out. "I am not one of them. They force me to work. I am in their debt."

"We're looking for a Bedouin with a black-and-white-checked *guttra*," Bolan said. "Where do they have him?"

"Please, English. He is at the house of Hussein, the eldest brother. I served him food not two hours ago."

"Then he's okay?" Bolan said.

The man nodded.

"Which house?" Grimaldi asked. "Which one is it?"

"The last house on the left."

"Did you hear them talk?" Bolan asked. "Are they expecting us?"

"It is—" he searched for a word, his eyes wild with fear "—strange to say. Hamza, a younger brother, is the one they listen to. He told them to set up an ambush here, then he sent out men to kill you some other place."

"So do they have an ambush set up here?"

"No. Here they don't have many men. Hussein took most of them to Umm al-Qulban earlier," the frightened servant blurted out.

"What do they plan here?" Grimaldi asked.

"The guards at the gate have been alerted, but they are lazy. Four men with rifles are in houses along the street. I don't know which ones."

"What about Hussein's house?" Bolan asked. "Do they have guards there?"

"One with the prisoner."

Bolan thought about the setup for a few minutes. It could have been a lot worse. He put aside the drugs and was about to give the Arab an hour or two of sleep with the butt end of his gun when he realized he might be passing up a great opportunity. Servants have ears like satellite dishes. "What are they planning?" he asked. "You can guarantee your life if you can tell us."

"Oh, English. It is very bad." The man was terrified. "They hate the Saudi princes. They have killed some and they will kill more. It is from the past, you see. The Saudis killed many of their ancestors."

"Where will they kill more Saudi princes? Will it be at the hajj?" Bolan asked.

"I do not know, English. If I knew I would tell you."

Bolan hit him on the side of the head with his gun butt. "Let's get out of here," he ordered. "We've got to get al-Murra."

When the leather case was back in Grimaldi's pocket, Bolan led him out of the house. "One phosphorus grenade in each house except this one and the one where they're holding al-Murra. Toss them in a front window. The women will be in the back. Let's get to the heart of each rathole," the Executioner said as he moved off.

They raced up the street, weaving from side to side, tossing phosphorus grenades as they went.

Fire poured from the meeting house and six others as they approached the last two. Rashidi men had jumped from the windows, some aflame, some with their fingers on chattering machine guns, only to be cut down by return fire.

Black-robed women streaked from the back of each house carrying children, all heading for the open front gate.

"Let's make this fast," Bolan shouted as he tossed the last grenade, which shattered the glass in the front room of the house across the street from Hussein's house. A solid crump sounded over the noise of screams. Fire burst from the front room.

They ran for the last house and dived through the windows, shattering glass and wooden frames. Bolan was on his feet, his Ultimax spouting flame. A lone Arab backed up, punched in the chest by a half-dozen shots. He fell out of the window and into the street.

The house smelled of death, the sickly sweet smell of a rotting corpse. The two soldiers looked at each other in the dim light. Had the servant lied to them? Was al-Murra dead after all?

They followed the odor to a back room.

Al-Murra was bound hand and foot on a bed of cushions in one corner. A bloated corpse lay crumpled in the opposite corner of the room.

Bolan slashed at the ropes with his commando knife and pulled al-Murra to his feet. The former SAS man had difficulty walking, but his rescuers had him out of the house in seconds. They paused at the base of the wall to let him rest and rub the rope marks.

"Who was the dead man?" Bolan asked.

"Just a kid who got in the way. He sat at my table at the teahouse," the Bedouin said sadly.

As they prepared to scale the back wall, a figure stumbled from the burning building, his robe in flames.

"Who's that?" Bolan asked. "Anyone we should talk to?"

"I think he's one of the brothers," al-Murra replied, still rubbing his wrists.

Bolan ran to the Rashidi and rolled him on the ground. The fire had consumed his robe and headdress and bits of cloth stuck to charred flesh.

The man was alive, and he looked at Bolan with hate-filled eyes.

"I heard them call him Hamza," al-Murra said. "One of the brothers."

"Tell me what you plan for the pilgrimage," Bolan ordered, holding the dying man by the shoulders.

"The wrath of Allah will rise up and smite the Sunni, and they will never rise again."

"But how do you plan to do it?" Bolan persisted.

He was talking to a dead man. The lidless eyes stared at him. The hate that had blanketed his charred features started to slip away as the face went slack.

"Great!" Bolan's frustration slipped into the open. "That man probably helped plan the whole deal and he's dead. We should have been more careful, gone slower."

"Sure, and you'd probably be dead in the street instead of him," Grimaldi said. "We've got al-Murra, and we live to fight another day. Hey. That's a profit in my book."

Sirens started to fill the night with their two-toned wail. They seemed to be coming from every direction.

"Let's get out of here," Grimaldi said.

When they were over the wall and in the truck, al-Murra accepted a cigarette from Grimaldi. "It's not all lost," he said, blowing smoke out the window. "I heard a few snatches of conversation back there. The rest of the brothers are at Umm al-Qulban. They're meeting with several ayatollahs and some foreigners from up north."

"When's the meet?"

"Not sure. Soon. The hajj is only a few days away."

Grimaldi was driving. "I'd like to check the bird over again," he said.

"She's all right."

"Just the same, I'd like to check on her," the pilot insisted.

"You're like a mother hen, you know that?" Bolan said. "Okay. Let's look at the bird, and then we get some sleep."

They found the weed-concealed plane without running into the patrols. The Cessna engine turned over with the slightest pressure on the button. The gas gauge showed she was more than half-full, enough to get them out.

"Okay. Satisfied?" Bolan turned to al-Murra. "Jack doesn't know what a Bedouin hotel is like. How'd you like to drive partway to Umm al-Qulban and find one?"

THE SMALL CONVOY of cars and trucks pulled into Umm al-Qulban at four in the morning. They'd had to stop to tend some of the wounded. The women had to tend to the children. When the attack came, three of the brothers who were away from the compound were supposed to be on their way to the northern fortress, but instead were in a house of pleasure that wasn't supposed to exist in an Islamic city. When they heard the sirens, they returned to the compound and found the death and destruction. With military patrols surrounding their compound, they'd organized the convoy.

Hussein met them at the huge steel gates, a guard at each elbow. "What is all this?" he bellowed at his brothers.

"The compound has been razed to the ground. Hamza is dead," one of the brothers said meekly.

"Hamza? Dead? How?" he asked, his face reflecting his murderous intent.

"Two figures in black. They moved so fast," one of the brothers said. He hadn't been there, but his wife had seen the whole attack.

"By two men?" Hussein stormed.

"We heard they were like devils," the same brother replied.

"You heard? Where were you?"

The three brothers looked at one another. Hussein's wrath would never end if he knew. "We were just starting to join you," another brother added to the story. "We turned back when we heard the explosions."

The big bearded man stood towering above them. "I will get them," he said in a voice that sent chills up their spines. "I'll get the swine that call themselves men, and when I get my hands on them they'll wish they could die quickly."

He turned, ignoring the others, and stormed through the gates.

The guards, left alone, followed one of the brothers inside. "What happened to Ahmed and Abdi and the rest of the guards?" one man asked.

"Dead. All dead," the brother said without breaking his stride.

The two guards looked at each other, fear stalking them like predators. They walked to the guards' quarters to pass the word.

THE TALL BEARDED CID CHIEF sat in his leather swivel chair and listened to his lieutenant.

"The Rashidi compound in Hail has been destroyed. Some of the brothers and a few guards were killed." Bindagii was shaking with excitement.

"Did we get a description of those responsible?"

"Vague. Two men dressed in black. One was tall, the other slightly shorter."

"The American. What is he up to now? Why the Rashidis?" Sedik asked, as if to himself. He shook himself and addressed Bindagii. "You notice anything special?"

"Not yet."

"That is why you are the aide and I the chief," the captain said. "He didn't hesitate to destroy the compound. He killed Rashidi men and their guards just as he did in Abu Dhabi. What about the women?"

"The fronts of the houses were set fire first. Not one woman or child was injured."

"It fits the pattern," Sedik speculated. "The man has a code of honor. Kill your enemies. Do not harm innocents. Leave the police strictly alone. I like this. I like it very much."

The lieutenant stood silent for once. They were talking about a master criminal who had killed a number of times. His boss was gloating as if he had the man in custody and was about to mete out punishment. He was puzzled.

"You still don't get it, do you?" Sedik asked.

Bindagii shook his head.

"A worthy opponent. A mystery," Sedik mused. "He murders the sheikh of Abu Dhabi, steals a plane, shows up again and turns the tables on our man Murshed but doesn't kill him. Then he attacks the most feared tribal leaders in the north. Why, Bindagii? How does it all fit together?"

"We had him, and he slipped away at the executions," Bindagii said, reciting the one fact his boss had left out. "He got away without firing a shot. His accomplice did all the killing."

"And the accomplice was killed in Abu Dhabi," Sedik added. "So where did he pick up the new accomplice to help him in Hail? Does he have an organization we don't know about?"

"What about a house-to-house search in Riyadh?" Bindagii suggested. "He has to have a safehouse here."

"No. He could be in one of the native hotels where we don't insist on passports or police cards. We could make many enemies in the search. Too many VIP households disturbed unnecessarily. No. We head for Hail, my friend."

"You don't seem to be in a hurry, sir."

"He will not be finished up north. I have a feeling he wants to talk to the Rashid brothers and he hasn't accomplished that yet," Sedik said. "We are in no hurry, Bindagii. The helicopter will get us there in less than two hours." He stood and came around the desk, stepping from the dais and clapping the younger man on the shoulder. "Patience, Bindagii," he said, feeling great, close to victory. "In this game the key word is patience."

11

The road out of Hail led them north. Al-Murra drove a
rented Toyota pickup to the small town of Al-Wuqid,
ten miles north of Hail. The small wreck of a vehicle
had been all they could get. He pulled up across from a
row of souks and left his friends while he made a few
purchases.

"New clothes for you," he said to the Americans
when he returned, tossing them two robes.

They pulled the robes over their dust-caked battle
dress and adjusted the *guttras* and *egals*. All three could
pass for Saudi men. The small Toyota was their ship of
the desert, but it was too hot to use as a base.

"How are you fixed for money?" al-Murra asked
Bolan.

"I have a few thousand riyals."

"Good. I can pick up a secondhand four-wheel-drive
vehicle and a few survival tools," the Bedouin said,
leading them to a native restaurant and leaving them
with steaming plates of chicken and rice.

"Is this all they eat here?" Grimaldi asked.

Bolan ignored the complaint.

"How long's he going to be?"

"I don't know, Jack. He knows what he's doing.
We're lucky to have him. We need a battle wagon for
Umm al-Qulban. If it was just you and me, we'd have

to steal the transport, and that leaves a trail. We've got a great ally in al-Murra, so let's leave it to him."

The Bedouin warrior was back in an hour with a battered Jimmy. It was so desert-weary you couldn't tell what the original color had been.

"What the hell's this?" Grimaldi asked.

"Bought it from a Korean who's the local mechanic here. Runs like a clock," al-Murra said. "It's also air-conditioned."

"Desert gear?" Bolan asked.

"Got a shovel, an air compressor and ten gallons of water," the Bedouin answered. "All I could manage in the time." He picked up half a chicken and tossed it into a plastic bag, scooped in some of the rice and twisted the bag closed. "I'll eat on the way. Let's go get the bastards."

UMM AL-QULBAN WAS NESTLED on one of the slopes of Jabal Aja, a range of hills just south of An-Nafud. It was a village of a hundred and fifty houses and perhaps three hundred families and seemed an unlikely place for the seat of Rashidi power. In centuries past Rashidi princes ranged hundreds of miles, gathering their supporters for raids on the Saudis and lesser tribes. It had been a way of life.

As their old Jimmy rolled into town, they could see the Rashidi palace, which was much larger than the other houses and the two mosques. Frescoed and turreted, it was of ancient Arab construction, at least three stories high, and was built of hardpan dirt molded like concrete. The government office building, low-slung and decrepit, was the smallest building in town. Like the others, it was surround by a high concrete wall.

They were in the camp of the enemy.

"We're too conspicuous," al-Murra told them. Dogs barked in their wake and the curious followed them as they drove down the one main street. "We'll take a pipe at the local hotel and try to keep the locals from joining us."

The local hotel was another like the one Jabbar had called a Bedouin hotel, a collection of rectangular wood frames for sleeping pallets all set out in front of a decrepit coffee house. The wood frames, held together by strips of reed, were about six feet by three, the cane bottoms raised far enough from the ground to discourage climbing scorpions. Travelers carried their own bedding. They rented the frames for one riyal a night.

At al-Murra's direction the proprietor filled three hookahs and lit them. The man pulled three frames into a U formation and accepted six riyals for his trouble. The three warriors would have some degree of privacy for less than the cost of a pack of cigarettes.

"You saw the fortress," al-Murra said softly. While not close to others, they were the center of attention.

"Looks formidable," Bolan said. "I doubt it can be stormed easily. Better do it at night."

"I agree," al-Murra said. "The dogs will have to be silenced. I haven't figured how to do that yet."

"I've never seen so many damned dogs," Grimaldi said. "What are they doing here?"

"It's a plague we've had to endure since most of the elite turned their hounds loose years ago," al-Murra remarked offhandedly. "They run wild in every community in the kingdom where they can feed on garbage."

"Why were they turned loose?" Grimaldi asked, taking a long drag on his pipe.

"A fair question. What they did sounds stupid and cruel now. The Saluki hound used to be favored for hunting. No one ever gave a thought to conservation, so all the animals the Saluki used to hunt were killed off. The princes turned to falconry and had no use for the dogs. They didn't think of the creatures as pets, so they were turned loose."

"Doesn't the population grow fast?" Grimaldi asked.

"It does. In the cities the local government poisons them about once a year."

"What about towns like this?" Bolan asked.

"I don't know what they do here," al-Murra admitted.

"We'll have to figure out how to get around that problem later," the Executioner said.

When they returned to the Jimmy, al-Murra was about to climb behind the wheel when a group of Rashidis, all carrying SMGs at the ready, encircled the truck. Al-Murra started to turn on them and was clubbed to the ground by a rifle butt. Bolan reached for his Beretta and was bringing it to bear when a club took him at the back of the skull. He went down, everything turning black. The last thing he remembered was the face of Grimaldi hitting the dirt beside him, blood pouring from shattered lips. His last fleeting thought was of the dogs. They were no problem now.

THE RASHIDI WAS FAT and ugly, his nose a piece of flat putty. His ears, sticking out from under a *guttra* thrown back to reveal a lace skullcap, were big and disfigured as if he'd spent years in the wrestling ring. His voice resembled the roar of a lion. He started to speak in Arabic, but when he saw he wasn't understood he switched to cultured English.

"Before we tear you apart, I want to know who you are," he rumbled, his massive voice filling the room.

"You are Hussein ibn-Abdul Azziz ibn-Rashid," al-Murra said.

The words were barely out of his mouth when a rifle butt struck him on the same spot he'd been hit when they were taken. He went down and stayed down. He didn't look good. His face was pasty; his breath was ragged.

"Don't tell them anything," Bolan told Grimaldi. He didn't try to whisper, and his voice carried throughout the room.

They were in a kind of throne room on the second floor. The walls were hung with posters of Saudi scenes, probably propaganda distributed by the Minister of the Interior. The floors were covered with expensive Persian rugs. Bolan had been conscious while they were dragged to the chamber. He had noted the route in detail and could find his way back to the front door and the inner compound if he had the chance. The trick was to stay alive and look for an opening.

"He was right," the voice boomed out of the fat man. "I am Hussein. It is my duty to rule the Rashidis and ultimately all of the peninsula."

"Why tell us?" Grimaldi asked.

"Because my brother Hamza is dead and you killed him," Hussein snarled. "They tell me he died in much pain, his flesh burned from him." The fat man's face was a storm cloud, and the knuckles gripping his chair arms were white. "Many of my men have died at your hand," the big man continued. "First you will tell us all we want to know, then we will disembowel you and burn your flesh while you watch. It will not be a pleasant death."

"What's the delay? You expecting company?" Bolan asked. It all added up. They were just waiting for the word, or the final details. Bolan was sure the Rashidis were only a small part of the plan. Maybe they were being used. If others were involved as he suspected, they had to show up here soon.

"You will feel my wrath soon enough, American," the big Arab said, the wattles of his cheeks shaking with rage. "You may tell your man not to talk, but it won't make any difference. When he feels the knife and sees his guts spilling from his body, and the hot coals brought closer, he'll tell us everything." He turned to his men. "Take them below and show them the first phase of our hospitality." Addressing Bolan, he said, "I'm sorry I will miss the entertainment. But I have more important things to do."

THE ROOM WAS small and dirty. Moonlight from a cloudless night shone through a few slits in the wall above Bolan's head. All three men were sprawled on the floor naked, their hands tied behind their backs. The guards had stripped them. They had been angered by the sight of the black clothing under the robes, so they were far from gentle. Out of sight of their leader, they had clubbed the three men senseless, smashing gun butts into yielding flesh long after their prisoners were unconscious.

Bolan recovered first and sat with his back to a dirt wall. He tried to examine his friends, but was restricted by his bonds. Al-Murra hadn't moved since the last time they had clubbed him. Grimaldi had taken the worst beating because he had taunted his captors instead of taking the punishment. They had broken one of his arms. The Executioner realized if he was able to make a break, neither man would be able to help him.

Bolan's bonds chafed at his wrists. He tried to get his fingers loose, but they slipped in the blood that seeped from deep gouges and made the ropes wet and unmanageable. As he continued to move his wrist through the pain, the blood acted as a lubricant. Gradually the pad of one thumb slipped through the hemp, followed by the other.

He stayed inert as a guard entered, looked them over, then left. Bolan heard them in the next room talking in Arabic, but he didn't understand enough of the garbled sounds to make out what they were saying. He strained to hear and thought his mind was playing tricks on him—women's voices speaking English in a room overhead! His imagination had to be working overtime.

Bolan's arms were cramped from being in the same position for so long. When the guard left, he pulled one arm to the front, then the other. He sat for a moment, stretching his muscles, confident that a guard wouldn't return soon.

Al-Murra groaned and opened his eyes, but his stare was unfocused. He wouldn't be of any help in a fight. Bolan knew that it would be up to him. A private war again. He found his dusty combat clothes tossed in a corner and pulled them on. Every inch of his body hurt where they had pounded him hours earlier.

The door to the room wasn't locked, and it opened onto the guards' chamber, not a hallway. Bolan peered through the slits in its wooden surface. Two guards sat in a dimly lit room. A bare bulb, probably twenty-five watts of power, lit the table but not the corners of the room. The men were eating. Their weapons were on the floor beside them.

Bolan opened the door slowly. The hinges complained, but the guards were engrossed in their meal. The Executioner flexed his wrists to get the blood flowing.

The room smelled of strong cologne. Like most peninsula Arabs, the men were clean but used too much male perfume. One man sat with his back to the door. His bulk concealed Bolan from the second man.

The Executioner streaked from the door to the first man, caught him behind the ear with a karate chop and jumped across the table to grasp the other man by the hair. It was a maneuver that had worked many times but not now. The man's *guttra* came away in his hand.

The Rashidi guard turned to reach for his gun, but Bolan had the man by the ears in a microsecond, smashing his forehead against the table. In a reflex action, as he went down, the Rashidi swung his rifle in an arc to catch Bolan in the groin. As the man's head hit the table like a ripe melon, searing streams of pain coursed up from Bolan's crotch, doubling him over.

The pain receded, starting with his head and finally descending to his gut. The pain never left his groin. He grabbed for the table with both hands and pulled himself up. No one had heard the struggle. If they had, he would have been surrounded by other guards by now.

Bolan looked around. The weapons the Rashidis had taken from them were on a small crate in one corner. He strapped on his shoulder holster, checked the Beretta's action, slid in a fresh magazine and holstered the weapon. He slung an AK over his shoulder and took two grenades from the webbing of the fallen Rashidi.

Before he sheathed his commando knife, he returned to the other room and cut his friends' bonds.

The door to an outer hall had a small window. A quick look through the glass revealed no one. He examined the two guards. The man he'd cracked against the table wasn't going to harm anyone for a long time. The other would have to be tied. He tended to them, covering his back, then catfooted into the corridor.

Dim bulbs lit the hallway and a staircase. He remembered seeing two massive diesel generators behind the structure, and he could hear the dull hum even now and feel the vibration of their action through the soles of his thin sandals.

One guard sat at the top of the staircase. The whole area was poorly lighted, but the warrior, even in commando black, would be seen long before he got to the top of the stairs. He eased the Beretta from its holster, the dull black metal shining faintly in the dim light.

He could nail the guard easily, but where would the man's body land? Would he be blasted off the chair and fall away from the blast, or would he fall down the stairs? Either way the fall would make too much noise.

As Bolan charged up the stairs, the guard twisted on his chair and brought up the Kalashnikov. Bolan fired, catching the guard a grazing shot in the head. The man wavered, then started to fall toward the stairs. Bolan caught him and sat him back on the chair.

No one else was around. The Executioner heard voices coming from a room at the end of a wide hallway. It was dark at the far end. He padded to the room and carefully eased himself toward the small glass window in the door.

Hussein Rashid sat at the end of the room, facing the door. Three men, who resembled him slightly, were also in the room. All four wore blue-and-white-checked *guttras*. Four of the Rashid brothers. Bolan knew there were eight, less the dead Hamza, so three others weren't present.

The other guests were a mixture. Three were high-ranking Soviets, which were given away by their clothing. They weren't dressed in the ill-fitting suits of the KGB. Rather, their clothes reflected the tailoring of the new Soviet elite's imitation of Savile Row. The style had started to show up since the ascendancy of Gorbachev. One of the three, foolishly, or to impress the other, wore the Order of Lenin on his left breast.

Three men were dressed in the dark brown robes and white headgear of Iranian ayatollahs. One looked familiar—a personality Bolan had occasionally seen on television. So this meet had to be very high-level. The warrior opened the door a crack and listened.

"...have rented a large compound in Mecca. Big enough to sleep three or four hundred," Hussein was saying.

"Like a hotel," one of the Soviets said.

"Our people do not sleep one to a room," one of the ayatollahs said. "It is a walled compound with four houses in it. Our people sleep on mattresses they can carry. It's the hajj. Most Muslims will be carrying their own sleeping and cooking gear."

"Where is it exactly?" another of the Soviets asked in badly accented English.

"You will never enter the holy city," an ayatollah answered. He was the one Bolan recognized from news broadcasts. "But it doesn't matter if you know the location," the Iranian went on. "It is within the Harram boundary, so it is very close to the Great Mosque."

"The Harram?"

"The most holy area surrounding the mosque. We are on Al-Shemeisy Street, the only pink compound on the street. Do not worry. We have enough men to abduct the king and his party. We have an imam, a holy man to sway the crowds. We will take the king and persuade the crowds to follow us. It will be a new wave of converts to the fundamentalist movement."

"I don't understand why the king will be vulnerable," one of the Soviets said. He was the one with the order pinned on his chest; he appeared to be in charge.

"You don't have to know the details. The king must make obeisance to Allah before each pilgrimage. It is the duty of the titular head of our faith," the senior ayatollah said, his mouth a grim line. "The Saudis usurped the honor when the murdering Ibn Saud captured the Hejaz and all of the western coast many years ago. They are unworthy. Our reward will be to take over the leadership and spread fundamentalism."

It sounded like a speech to Bolan, but then it always did when fanatics were turned loose. If he could learn the Soviet motive, he'd have it all.

"Our man must succeed the king," the Soviet leader reminded them.

"Prince Sultan will be declared king in the next day or two," the ayatollah said. The senior one was the only one to speak now. The others seemed content to let him take the lead. "When we have control of the Harram and Islamic fundamentalism is recognized as the power behind the Islamic world, we will kill Sultan and your man Prince Bandar will replace him."

"My people want control of Saudi oil without going through your country to get it," the Soviet confirmed. "If this works out, my people agree that we can be allies in other projects."

"Two things we want. Half the Saudi oil output will be ours," the ayatollah said. "In addition, we want help with the Iraqi war. The Syrians can attack on the western flank. You control them. We could take Iraq in days."

"This is no time for new conditions, comrade," the Soviet admonished, obviously annoyed. It was exactly the kind of negotiating that the Soviets had pulled for years. They were familiar with the tactic but had seldom been on the receiving end. "I would have to inform my people of this. They understand our original plan as we discussed it previously. We have no time for change."

"In this day of electronic marvels, you have time. You have plenty of time," ayatollah said, his expression emotionless.

Bolan had heard enough. Too much. The enemy plans he'd heard put him in the position of both a politician and a warrior. If the men in this room were to die now, the uprising and attempted kidnapping would probably continue and that would be the extent of it. If they were to successfully negotiate a more complicated deal, the whole Iran-Iraq war would be affected, Syria would no longer be a closet Soviet state, and a path to Saudi oil fields would be blazed through Iraq.

Characteristic of the Executioner, he decided quickly. He didn't know if other Rashidis might be at his back now or if they would show up soon. He pulled the pin on one of his antipersonnel grenades, counted to five, opened the door wide and tossed the grenade onto the middle of the table. The last thing he saw as he dived for cover was the startled look on the faces around the table. They seemed frozen in fear, unable to move.

The blast blew the door off at the moment Bolan hit the floor. The heavy slab of wood sailed over his head and down the stairs. Bolan had the AK off his shoulder and spitting flame in 3-round bursts at the guards below as they poured into the lower hall. The men were cut down, stacked on top of one another like kindling, their blood against the backdrop of white robes a contrasting splash of crimson.

With a short pause in the action, Bolan raced down the stairs to the room where he'd left his friends.

12

Grimaldi cradled his broken arm against his body. Al-Murra was sitting with his head in both hands, disoriented, his stare blank.

Bolan pulled them both to their feet and got them moving. He grabbed their clothes, and as he slung a couple of AKs over his left shoulder, he herded them out to the hall and a rear exit.

A beat-up Nissan truck sat in the boiling sun near the back door.

"Take one of these," he shouted at them, tossing each an AK-47. They might be hurting, but they were soldiers and their work was fighting, not nursing wounds.

He'd never been so right in his life. As they headed for the door, a half-dozen men rounded a corner of the building and opened fire. If they hadn't been poor shots, they would have scythed the trio down. Bolan had his arms full of clothing, but Grimaldi opened fire despite his bad arm. His stream of tumblers brought down two Rashidis. The others scrambled for cover behind the house.

Bolan managed to get his charges into the back of the truck and out of the compound before the surviving guards could mount a chase. He chose to stick close to the hills to the northwest, knowing the search for them

would center around the more traveled routes to the
south. He hadn't covered a mile before a plume of dust
behind them signaled pursuit. He should have known
he'd be seen. It was almost impossible to get away
without leaving a trail. Powdered hardpan curled behind the Nissan truck, setting up a cloud worse than
that of his pursuers.

The warrior knew Grimaldi still had a few rounds left
in his clip. Al-Murra hadn't fired his weapon. Bolan had
a few rounds in the clip of his assault rifle. He had one
grenade left and eight rounds in his automatic. It would
have to do.

Their pursuers gained on them quickly. In his side-
view mirror Bolan could see a half-dozen men in the
vehicle behind. When they closed to about a hundred
yards, he felt a few 7.62 mm slugs tear into the bucking
Nissan. He couldn't hear the enemy for the noise he was
making.

The Rashidi truck came on. They ran a parallel
course twenty feet away, and even at that distance, with
both trucks bumping through rough terrain, their gun-
ners couldn't score a vital hit. Bolan pulled the pin on
a grenade and held the firing pin down with the inside
of his arm pressed to his side while he tried to bring his
own AK to bear. It was almost impossible to score a hit,
like two skiers on a slalom run trying to shoot at each
other. The road was rutted, and Bolan had to use both
hands to steer most of the time.

The Rashidi truck swerved closer, bringing it to
within ten feet. Most of the enemy guards were awk-
wardly trying to change clips. Bolan let the grenade
drop from his armpit to his left hand, tossing it under-
hand in one fluid motion. It hit one of the men in the
chest and dropped to the floor of the truck.

They all saw it coming. Their eyes swiveled to where it lay. In a panic the driver veered sharply. Three seconds later the Rashidi truck blew into a ball of red and orange flame. The Executioner slowed and turned to see the result. Men were strewn along the dirt track, torn and aflame. As he left them in his wake, none of the enemy were standing.

FIVE OR SIX MILES farther along the road, Bolan stopped to give his compatriots in the rear of the truck a few minutes to change their clothes and recover. Grimaldi had been hit in the shoulder of his bad arm and sat trying to stem the flow of blood. Al-Murra had taken a slug in the abdomen. It had missed vital organs and passed through his flank on the left side. Both holes oozed a thin stream of dark red blood.

The Executioner had learned most of the intelligence he needed to stop the Shiite plot, but he'd just lost a major battle. His two allies were out of action, and he had to get medical help for them. He had to get hold of Brognola again. Did the big Fed want him to tackle the Mecca compound or turn it over to the authorities?

He thought of the many times he'd tackled Mafia strongholds and come away the winner, leaving the enemy destroyed. This was a little different. The invasion of the holy Harram by a foreigner was a crime the Saudis would never forgive. They would probably applaud the action by a Muslim but would condemn an American even though he saved their skins. Politics tied his hands again, he thought, along with deeply held religious beliefs. Besides, he still had the problem of getting there, and he knew there would be roadblocks at every entry point into the holy city. He thought of going in by foot but knew the whole area was surrounded by almost impassable mountains.

While these thoughts ran through his weary brain, he tore strips from the bottom of robes and bound the wounds of his men. "How do you feel?" he asked Grimaldi as he worked.

"I've felt better," the flyer admitted, holding his throbbing arm.

"I don't have anything for pain," Bolan said. "I'll try to get some help for you."

"If I can get a cast on this, I'll be as good as new," the pilot replied.

"Sure you will. Forget about the war, Jack. You've just been awarded the Purple Heart. I'll need you later. We'll try to get you patched up and strong enough to fly us out."

He turned to al-Murra. The Bedouin hadn't spoken, even to complain as Bolan had patched him up. His eyes were blank as if they held a void behind them. He was out of it.

Bolan helped them back into the truck and struck out again, putting miles between them and the fortress at Umm al-Qulban. He saw movement in the distance straight ahead. A Bedouin encampment was taking shape in front of him about six miles to the east.

The desert wanderers had used old pieces of scrap metal sheeting and discarded wooden panels to fence off an area for their goats. It was a crude but effective corral. They were living in a few shacks made of the same material and also had a collection of black-and-white goatskin tents that were coated with the dust kicked up by the traffic of their trucks. Bolan had seen camps like it before, housing probably one family, three or four generations all living together.

He approached carefully. The men of the small settlement surrounded the truck. An old man, most likely the patriarch, and five young men stood in front, their families behind. They held no guns.

"*Salaam aleku,*" the old man said.

"*Aleku salaam,*" Bolan replied.

The old man made a long, impassioned speech.

Bolan didn't understand all of it. He felt a hand on his shoulder. Al-Murra's touch was tentative; his eyes still weren't clear. "He says you are...welcome to sit and eat with them. He has noticed...that we have wounded...he offers his best medicine women to help," al-Murra said, his effort painful. "He seems genuine. What he offers is very generous."

Bolan had seen generosity offered as a stalling tactic before while someone called the enemy. He was alive because he was careful. "Are you sure?" he asked.

"The Bedouin are...very seldom hostile to strangers. You were at my camp. You saw."

"But that was different."

"Not necessarily," al-Murra offered, grimacing as pain from the tear in his flank attacked him. "Maybe these people hate the Rashidis."

"Tell them we're glad of the help."

THE PATH up the steep slope was almost impossible for wounded men to manage, but they had chosen the impossible route instead of taking a chance on other routes that were heavily patrolled by Rashidis. The Bedouin, members of the local Shammar tribe, had been more than generous. They had provided them with three donkeys, refusing Bolan's money until he insisted. They gave the three warriors enough dried food and goatskins of water to make it over the high hills and to the desert on the other side. The three would have to follow the hills to the south and approach Hail via a circuitous route. Bolan didn't like it, but he had no choice.

The women, shy at first, had worked wonders with the wounded men. Grimaldi was in reasonably good shape. Al-Murra was running a fever. Bolan had them both secured to the donkeys. He checked on them as often as he could.

They reached the peak and started the treacherous descent at noon while the sun was at its zenith. In the early afternoon Bolan made camp on the lower slope of the hills to give the two wounded men an opportunity to rest. They wouldn't have the strength to ride all day.

Grimaldi and al-Murra were wrapped in blankets the Bedouin had graciously pressed on them. Bolan curled up in a blanket as the sun retreated behind the hills, but he couldn't sleep. He kept an eye on his charges hour after hour. He'd have to get them out of there soon. While Grimaldi was better than he'd been at the Rashidi fortress, neither man was in good shape.

Grimaldi grunted in his sleep and rolled to one side, his good hand reaching for his hip. When Bolan saw something scurry away, he shrugged off his blanket and gave chase. A large scorpion tried to crawl into a crevasse, but the warrior crushed it.

Bolan examined the small wound on Grimaldi's hip, which had turned red and started to swell. He felt helpless. He cut an X across the sting, squeezed out as much venom as he could and applied a dressing. He could do nothing more. The sun had been below the horizon for more than an hour and Bolan finally began to nod. He hadn't really slept in days, and he was dead tired.

At the feel of the cold steel on his forehead, he jerked awake and scrambled for his Beretta. A voice growled at him in Arabic, and the pressure of the muzzle increased.

He didn't understand the dialect, but the meaning was clear, so he froze, waiting for the next move. The man was outlined against the light of the moon, big and lean, and radiating a sense of power, strength.

"Who are you?" the stranger demanded finally in passable English.

"A pilot. We have a contract to spray crops for the Ministry of Agriculture." Bolan stuck to his cover story.

"Two of you wounded in a district with no crops? Where is your plane? Where are the crops?" the stranger snapped at him.

Bolan had said all he was going to say. From now on he would listen and wait for a break.

The man withdrew the gun from Bolan's forehead, then used his free hand to lift the soldier's handgun out of its holster. That accomplished, he kicked the AKs out of the reach of the other two men.

Bolan was able to see him better as he stepped back and the faint moonlight caught his rugged features. He was dressed in a safari suit with patch pockets. He wore a full *guttra* with the usual black two-band *egal* holding the cloth close to his head. A slight wind tugged at the long ends of the *guttra*, waving them away from his shoulders like small wings. A scar ran from his bearded chin to his forehead on the left side. Otherwise he would have been handsome.

The stranger squatted in front of Bolan, holding the rifle pointed in his general direction. He was just far enough away to prevent an attack and close enough to make it impossible to miss. The rifle was an old M-1. Bolan hadn't seen one in a long time.

"Word travels fast even here," the man said, his voice strong, his words too distinct to be his native tongue. "The Rashidi stronghold has been badly damaged. Three of the Rashid brothers, several of their guards and a few VIP visitors were killed. You wouldn't know anything about that, would you?"

Bolan couldn't figure the man. He could be on either side. If he'd been a Rashidi supporter, they would have been dead by now. He decided the man was either indifferent or was against the Rashidis. Whichever, he and his companions were better off than he'd thought at first.

"How did your friends get their wounds?" the stranger asked.

Bolan was still unwilling to open up. He didn't have time to spare, but with a gun on him he wasn't about to rush anything.

"I heard some of the Rashidis chased the attackers and ended up dead. You have any idea how many men the Rashidis lost?" the stranger continued, his questioning relentless. "It was twenty-two. Can you imagine how Rashid brothers feel? Twenty-two. Add that to the loss of Hamza and eight of his men in Hail and they're paranoid."

Bolan looked straight at the man and through him, his eyes slitted. He still kept his silence.

"Any man who could hurt them so bad is a friend of mine," the stranger said.

Bolan still wasn't biting.

"I am Salman Turbah," the man introduced himself, putting down his gun and placing the Beretta on the rock between them. "I am a Shammar. My people have lived here for centuries."

Bolan reached for the gun. He chambered a round and pointed the weapon at Turbah. "I take it you're not a friend of the Rashidis." He held the gun rock-steady, pointing at the Arab's head.

"When the Saudis defeated the Rashidis and killed off most of their men, the Rashidis took it out on neighboring tribes. Islamic rape and torture. It's against the laws we live by." He paused for a moment. "I have lost many uncles, cousins and brothers to their raids."

"I thought murder was punished by the sword," Bolan said, releasing the hammer of his gun and holstering it.

"Who's to know what goes on up here?" Turbah shrugged. "The Saudis govern well, but they don't bother with a handful of Rashid brothers. Most of the Rashidis accepted Ibn Saud's amnesty back in the twenties and early thirties when he took over all of the peninsula. They're strong supporters now. Why should the Saudis bother with the few who are left?"

"How do you feel about the Saudis? What do you know about their recent deaths?" Bolan asked.

"I spent four years in the army and two in the national guard. I'd be happier if they cleaned out the Rashidi rat's nest."

Bolan looked at the big man squatting in front of him and liked what he saw. He was a fighting man and a man in control. Maybe he could help in some way.

"Who are your friends?" Turbah asked.

"One is Adnan al-Murra, a Bedouin from the Rub' al-Khali. The other is Jack Grimaldi, a pilot and a friend." He described their wounds.

"Where is the scorpion you killed?" Turbah asked.

Bolan showed him the dead creature.

"A brown one," the Shammar pronounced after examining the scorpion. "He's lucky. He'll be a sick man for a few days. If it had been a lighter color he'd have been close to death by now."

"It's bad enough. Jack's been hit in the shoulder and he's got a broken arm. Al-Murra has a concussion and a couple of holes in his flank."

"Let's get them to my camp. It's just a mile from here." Turbah stooped to al-Murra, caught him in a fireman's lift and started down the rocky incline.

THE DOCTOR PULLED a syringe out of Grimaldi's flank and threw it into a waste container. "He'll be all right in a few days. I've taken out the bullet in his shoulder and the wound is clean. I'll put a cast on the arm before I go."

"What about the concussion?" Bolan asked. "I don't like the fact Adnan's been out of it for so long."

"I agree. I'd like X rays. We'll have to get them both to Hail as soon as possible."

"No. Turbah thinks we should lie low."

"No problem, Mr. Ford. My clinic's private. No one questions my comings and goings." The man, Dr. Wahhab Sharaf, was a Saudi who had been a student in North America half of his life. He was a friend of the Shammars and had no use for the Rashidis.

"We'll bring them in tomorrow night," Turbah said. "Your back door two hours after sunset."

"They'll be all right until then. I've left medication with your women."

When the doctor had gone, Bolan sat with Turbah around a smoking fire. He had met the patriarch Ahmed Noor Turbah and a few of his warriors. The elder

Turbah reminded him of Adnan's father—both tough old men who had roamed the desert most of their lives. They were sunbaked and desert-hardened, the survivors of privation and struggle. Unlike the elder al-Murra, the Turbah patriarch wasn't close to the royal family, but his loyalties were just as strong. Through his son he made his feelings clear.

"He wants to know what the Rashidis were up to and how he can help," Salman said. His father's English was poor, but he insisted on trying.

"Who were the men with the hated Rashidis?" the elder Turbah asked.

Bolan decided to let them have the whole story. What did he have to lose? They would know the timing and maybe they could find a way to help.

"The Shiites are evil," the venerable leader of the Turbah family said afterward. "They have tried to obtain dominance of the Islamic world for many years. Do you know the history?"

"Not the details."

"I will not bore you with it all," the older man said. His son was content to sit at his father's feet and listen. "The Shiites preach fundamentalism, a return to the cleaner, purer way of life. That is a false front. Beneath their facade they are evil. The concepts of Mohammed are not their concepts.

"We follow the Wahhabi teachings as do the Saudis. Mohammed ibn-Abdul Wahhab was an Islamic scholar in the eighteenth century. He persuaded the Saudis that the ways of Mohammed were pure and the only way to live their lives. The harsh teachings were taken to heart, and the writings of the Koran became civil law. It is still so."

"I've heard that," Bolan conceded. "How harsh is it?"

"No alcoholic drinking allowed. The purity of the marriage. The faces of women should not tempt men or take their minds away from the worship of Allah. Much good has come from Mohammed's teachings. Men who know the truth smile and follow the word. Those who do not know of his frailties follow blindly. In the end we are all better for it."

"So it comes down to a struggle between good and evil."

"You have a habit of getting to the heart of a situation, my friend," the old man said. "We will do anything to thwart the Shiites in this or any scheme for power. You have all of my men."

"That won't be necessary, sir," Bolan assured him. "But if you're volunteering help, I could use your son."

"If you are the man who led the raids on the Rashidi compound in Hail, I'm your man," Turbah said.

Bolan wasn't about to catalog his actions. He held out his hand and shook the Shammar's. The grasp was strong.

WHEN THE NEWCOMERS were asleep, Turbah sat apart from the tents, looking out over the land be loved. He remembered the stories his father had told him about the Rashidis and the brutal treatment they had handed out to the Shammars after the Saudis had taken over. It was before his time, but the deep hatred was as strong in him as in previous generations.

His father had never told him, but he'd learned from other elders of the tribe that his mother had been raped. She had almost died. It was a miracle that she was able to give birth to him and his brothers after her recovery.

How could a man not hate the Rashidis after such a history? He had grown to manhood and joined the national guard to learn the techniques of fighting. He'd been blooded, gravely wounded, and returned home a hero, ready to face his destiny at last. But he had been alone. The older men had changed, become passive. Many of the young ones had gone to the city to work and make their fortunes. He was out of place, a throwback, the only one equipped to take vengeance, but a man without allies.

His father had forbidden him to rouse the other young men to raid the Rashidis. It had been a way of life in generations past, but they were few in number now. The elder Turbah did not want to see his people decimated, his beloved sons killed.

But the tide had turned. The American had given his father incentive. The warrior had already done massive damage to the hated Rashidis. Now was the time to strike.

13

"I'm not crazy about this whole deal," Grimaldi grumbled as he lay on one side to avoid some of the discomfort. The wound in his shoulder was bothering him and his swollen hip throbbed painfully. "What the hell bit me, anyway?"

"Just a little bug. Quit complaining," Bolan said. "It could be worse."

"Yeah? How could it be worse?"

"You could be dead."

They were alone in front of a tent apart from the others. The desert air had turned cool. Turbah had lit a fire for them from some of the wood the Bedouin cherished so much in the desert clime. The sky was clear. Not a single cloud disturbed the spectacular display of stars. The Saudi air force base miles to the west lit the sky like the glow from a small city.

"It's this place, you know?" Grimaldi went on. "I don't understand a word they say. The place is crawling with poisonous things. You can't sit down safely."

"You're feeling sorry for yourself. That's not like you," Bolan observed. "This country has fewer dangerous animals than any place you've ever been. Honduras had to be twice as bad. You were just unlucky, is all."

"Yeah. I guess it's not just that. I don't see why we're into this. I've been shot, stung by something, and I don't see why we're fighting for these guys."

Bolan remembered that Brognola had parachuted Grimaldi into the action too fast. He didn't have papers, hadn't even been briefed. No wonder he was unhappy.

"Okay," the warrior conceded, knowing it was time for an overdue briefing. "You know we can't let the Soviets control the Persian Gulf. Everyone knows we can't let them control Middle East oil."

"Yeah. Anybody knows that."

"Well, they've got their noses into this," Bolan explained. "What's happened is that the people around the Ayatollah Khomeini have taken advantage of a feud between the Saudis and the Rashidis. The Iranians are like the Soviets in one way. The Reds want to convert the whole world to communism. The Iranians want to force the whole Islamic world to think their way."

"So?"

"The ayatollahs aren't able to see that the Soviets will eat them alive if this action goes down. And get the oil reserves, as well."

"You mean you, al-Murra and I are taking on the combined forces of the Soviets *and* the Iranians?"

"Not quite. I know who's been killing off the Saudi royal family now. Their plan is to create an incident at the next Islamic pilgrimage, kidnap the new Saudi king and put a puppet on the throne to replace him. They'll have maybe two or three hundred people at Mecca."

"So what does that do to us?"

"The puppet king will be friendly to the Soviets and the Iranians. They'll control him and through him most of the Middle East oil."

"So he won't be friendly to America."

"Right. Sounds elementary, but that's about it."

"You think we can stop them?"

"We? You're not going anywhere, friend. I'll need you to fly us out. Brognola has made it clear that we're out in the cold. The Saudis don't know we're here. One or two members of the royal family agreed to have us try our hand, but the ones who knew of the commitment could be dead now for all I know. We do our job, then get out."

"I hate jobs like that. You get out of line and you could even have the local police on your tail."

The ghost of a smile tugged at the corners of Bolan's lips. He was sitting cross-legged while Grimaldi lay on his side across the fire from him. He could see the expression on his friend's face through the flames. Grimaldi was still unhappy.

"Oh, no," the pilot said. "I know that look. You're telling me you're already in trouble with the police, right?"

"You can't have everything, pal. Let's get some shut-eye. We'll need it."

Grimaldi wasn't about to be put off. "How long until this pilgrimage starts?"

"I'm not sure, maybe next week. I'll check tomorrow."

"You're taking al-Murra to the doctor tomorrow, right? We'll see what he says. I'm going to be a part of this."

"We'll talk tomorrow."

Bolan lay down by the fire and pulled a blanket around him. He needed Jack. He had a plan in mind for Mecca, and he'd need one or two good men to help. Al-

Murra didn't qualify. Grimaldi was doubtful. Maybe
he'd have to have that talk with Brognola.

EVERYTHING HAD GONE WRONG that could go wrong.
Captain Sedik sat in the Toyota four-wheel-drive and
grumbled. "Where are we now? My rump feels like a
raw piece of meat."

"We're approaching Mudhnib. It's thirty miles to
Anaiza and another twenty to Burida," Lieutenant
Bindagii replied. "Why don't we sleep at Buraida to-
night? We'd be in Hail by noon the next day."

"The way things have been going we could have a
breakdown with this stupid truck like we did with the
damned helicopter."

"Just bad luck, Captain. It isn't the end of the
world."

"No? We have a breakdown with the helicopter just
as we were taking off. The military won't release one to
us. Damned jealous of us, that's why," Sedik complained. "Then the air-conditioning in this pile of junk
quits when we're just too far out of Riyadh to turn
back."

"We could have turned back," Bindagii suggested.

"Shut up and drive. We'll stay in Buraida for a few
hours, but I want to be in Hail early tomorrow."

"I don't see the urgency. We're not even sure the incidents in Hail and Umm al-Qulban had anything to do
with the American. Our local people could have handled it."

"Our local people are idiots, and you know it." Sedik pulled another cheroot from a crushed pack and lit
it. The smoke would have filled the cab, but the windows were open to offset the cruel temperature on the
highway. "I know the American is at the bottom of

both attacks. But why the Rashidis? It was one of their cousins the American killed in Abu Dhabi. What does he have on the Rashidis?'' Sedik asked, directing the question at himself rather than Bindagii. "The bastards aren't very popular, especially with the royal family, but what's the American got against them?"

"He's probably killed off the royal brothers and now he's started on the Rashidis," Bindagii offered facetiously. He often needled his boss, offering outlandish explanations to provoke argument, but his comments sometimes backfired.

"You could be right. We'll put the bastard out of action and the trouble we've been having will probably be over."

Bindagii drove on through the blistering heat. He didn't say anything more. He'd said too much already.

THE DOCTOR'S OFFICE, as Turbah promised, was on the outskirts of town and quite private. Bolan sat in an examining room with Grimaldi on one gurney and al-Murra on the other. Salman Turbah sat mute in a chair in the corner of the starkly white room. He observed everything that went on, but said nothing.

Dr. Sharaf walked out of his radiology room carrying three X rays. He slapped them into a viewer. "The concussion isn't serious. I'd like to keep al-Murra in bed here for a couple of days. Then he might be able to go back with you, but he'd still need bed rest."

"When will he be talking and reacting normally?" Bolan asked.

"In a couple of days."

"What about the bullet wounds?"

"No problem. The infection's cleaned up. He should heal fast."

"How dangerous would it be for him to travel?"

"Not a good idea. He probably wouldn't die from it, but any kind of extensive travel would slow his progress."

"How about flying?" Bolan asked.

The doctor looked at him with a jaundiced eye. "I'm no fool, Mr. Ford. I can guess who was involved in the Rashidi troubles. That's not my concern. I don't want this man traveling, and I especially don't want him within a mile of any gunfire."

Bolan had left his chair when the doctor entered. He had been looking over his shoulder when the X rays were illuminated. Now they stood eye to eye. Two strong-willed men bent on their own ends.

"Okay," Bolan said. "I just wanted the whole picture. What about Grimaldi?"

"Mr. Grimaldi is a different story. The bite is a minor discomfort. The poison will have passed through his system in a couple of days. The broken bone is only a minor inconvenience. I'm concerned about the shoulder wound," the doctor said, sitting beside Turbah and lighting a cigarette. "Too much action could open it up. He could end up with infection."

"But it's not life-threatening, right?"

"No, not if he's careful."

"All right!" Grimaldi said. "That means I can go with you to—"

"That's all I need to know, Doctor," Bolan interrupted. "And thanks for your help."

"And your silence," Turbah said, joining in for the first time.

"You're welcome. You can use this room for a few minutes if you like. I have other patients to see."

Bolan started to rise, but Turbah waved him down. "Why have you been ignoring me?" he asked.

"What do you mean?"

"You'd take Adnan if he was better. You're going to take Jack even thought he has only one arm. Am I a cripple?"

"This isn't your fight," Bolan said.

"I'm not a fool, Ford. I hear and I listen." He swiveled in his chair to face the American and made sure he had eye contact. "The Rashidis have been my enemies all my life. They've killed off some of the royal family, men I loved and admired. I overheard you tell Grimaldi that they're involved with the Soviets and the Iranians. Any fool can see what they could bring."

He sat silent for a moment, letting Bolan digest his outburst. "I'm trained," he went on. "I'm as good a man as you can find to help."

"You don't even know what's involved," Bolan said. "It won't be a piece of cake. Maybe three men against two hundred or more."

"So?"

"So when was the last time you killed a man?" Bolan growled, maintaining the eye contact.

"In 1979 I was in the national guard when the Shiites took over the Great Mosque in Mecca. You never read it in the newspapers, but we lost three hundred men to their hundred and fifty. They were dug in and we were in the open. I took three slugs in the thighs, but I got as much as I gave."

"Welcome to the team," Bolan said. "What we're into here is the sequel to your 1979 battle."

"What do you mean?"

"Apparently you didn't hear everything, my young friend. The action will be in Mecca again. But this time we're going to make sure it doesn't get as far as the Great Mosque."

"Okay!" the young Shammar shouted.

"When does the new king perform his obeisance in the Kabah?"

"On the first day. That would be four days from now."

"Then we hit them in three days."

"We hit them? The three of us?" Grimaldi asked.

"Unless you fall apart in the meantime."

Grimaldi grinned his response.

"One thing," Bolan concluded. "You tell no one about the where and when. We take Adnan to your father's tent and we fly to Mecca. That's it."

The door suddenly burst open and two uniformed men rushed into the room, holding guns. Captain Sedik smiled for the first time in days as he moved closer and waved Bolan to the wall.

Lieutenant Bindagii holstered his gun, approached Bolan and Turbah and patted them down. Two national guardsmen entered and trained their rifles on the group.

"An interesting little toy," Sedik commented as Bindagii removed Bolan's gun from its holster. "You can say goodbye to it. You won't be needing it again."

They were paraded through the clinic to the front door where a crowd had gathered. As they passed along the hall, Bolan could see that Dr. Sharaf was on the floor of his office, a trickle of blood oozing from a scalp wound. One of the troopers was trying to drag him to his feet.

They were herded into two black vans that were like ovens in the midday heat. Bolan and Turbah, the most dangerous, rode in one van. Grimaldi, al-Murra and the doctor shared the other.

It took less than ten minutes for the ride from the clinic to the national guard post, but it was long enough. The heat was suffocating.

THE FORTRESS at Umm al-Qulban was a beehive of activity, not all of it productive. The action was accompanied by a lot of shouting, most of it from the cavernous mouth of Hussein Rashid. He had a turban bandage on top of his head instead of the *guttra* he usually wore. One arm was in a sling, and he used a crutch to get around.

Ten or more men were working on the second floor where the explosion had taken place. They threw damaged material through a hole in the shattered exterior wall.

"You should rest," one of Hussein's surviving brothers said. "It is a miracle that you are alive."

"It is the will of God, Mahad," Hussein said humbly, his voice a mere whisper compared go his normal volume. Mahad was his favorite brother, even more so than the brilliant Hamza. He had protected the younger man from harm since they were boys. "Are the others all accounted for?"

"The bodies of the Soviets were collected this morning. Their embassy people were notified by private messenger."

"And the Iranians?"

"A truck arrived this morning to collect the bodies. I don't know where it came from and I don't care," the younger man replied. "The Soviets must have reported the deaths to them. No one from here would contact them."

"I know the devil who did this." Hussein's voice contained all the menace the big man could muster. "That tall Westerner with dark hair."

"We'll probably never see him again," Mahad said. "We won't go to Mecca now, and he'll be out of the kingdom."

"Don't bet on it. A man like that will not give up. If he knows about Mecca, he will be there and I will get my hands on him."

"Buy surely... I don't... Surely you're not going ahead now? Not after this."

"By Allah, you don't think like a true Rashid at all. I've been too soft on you. Of course we will be at Mecca. I want to see the king humbled. I want to be there to claim our birthright," he shouted. "You think I'd let the stinking Soviets and the lying Iranians take over the show? No way, my brother. You and I and all of ours will be there."

THEY WERE QUESTIONED separately, and Sedik left Bolan to the last. It was probably a psychological ploy but it wouldn't make any difference.

Grimaldi came back first, his face a mask of pain. They had hacked at his cast and poked at his shoulder bandage. He dropped to the floor beside Bolan and simply shook his head. He hadn't told them anything.

Turbah was next. He returned with one eye closed and a split lip. They had beaten him about the abdomen with rubber tubes. He, too, had been unwilling to talk. He simply gave Bolan a look that confirmed his silence, then sprawled on the floor beside Grimaldi.

While al-Murra was gone—and when the other two could speak—Bolan questioned them about what they had seen. How many rooms? How many guards? He gathered a wealth of information. Al-Murra returned to the room with no visible signs of brutality marring his flesh.

By the time they got around to Bolan the day was spent. It was dark outside. A moonless night left an invisible blanket over the northern city. Sedik was in an expansive mood. He had bested the man he'd been seeking for days. He could see commendation and promotion in the near future. He had changed his mind about promotion. With position went power. It was time he moved up. He might not have the daily excitement of the chase, but he'd get a larger slice of the pie and he could develop other interests.

The two officers sat at a small round table. An empty chair awaited Bolan on the other side. One guard stood at the door, holding an M-16 assault rifle.

Bolan scanned the room, his eyes missing nothing. The lieutenant, keeping his distance, had his service revolver on the table in front of him. Sedik played with the Beretta, caressing its sleek lines, tossing it into the air and catching it in a poor imitation of a Western gunslinger. The Executioner decided the CID man must be very pleased with himself.

Bolan also noted that his gun still had a clip in it, but that didn't mean anything. The clip could be empty. The Beretta could be a carrot for Bolan to jump at. He also noted that the lieutenant's revolver was loaded; at least the chambers he could see had rounds in them.

Sedik was in for a surprise. Bolan had warned the others not to talk, but he intended to talk himself. He had to know if the police suspected his motives. He had to know if they would believe he was on their side. He couldn't trust the others to try the same ploy, to tell half-truths, to learn more than he was willing to give.

"Just who do you think I am?" he asked. The question threw them off. They had expected to be on the offensive.

"We know who you are," Sedik replied with confidence.

"Oh?"

"You killed Abdul Rachman Rashid in Abu Dhabi. You killed Hamza Rashid in Hail. Allah only knows how many you killed in Umm al-Qulban," Sedik countered, not as sure of himself as he'd been before.

Like many police forces, the CID men had used plastic tape instead of handcuffs to restrain their prisoner. The plastic worked well in most situations. In Saudi Arabia, in this room, with the temperature at a hundred even at this hour, the plastic softened.

"Have I killed one of yours?" he asked.

This had nagged at Sedik and still did.

"One of my men was killed at the pesticide camp."

"I had nothing to do with that."

"This is madness. You are one of the worst criminals I've seen since I joined the force," Sedik shouted. "I will do the questioning here."

Bolan kept his cool. "I've killed only enemies of the Saudis. On the approval of certain royal princes, I might add."

"And who are the princes who approved this? Am I to believe they would prefer you to me?"

"They must. Their brothers are still dying," Bolan countered.

"And I suppose you have solved the problem?" Sedik asked sarcastically, his face taking on a light purple hue.

Bolan noted that Bindagii was intrigued. The guard was absorbed. Sedik was furious. "I know who plans to try for a coup," Bolan said, easing forward in his chair.

"Nonsense. I know Americans. You'll blame it on the Soviets."

"And the Rashidis."

Sedik laughed, rocking back and forth in his chair. "Eight brothers and a few followers?" Sedik managed through his laughter.

The plastic slipped over the Executioner's wrists. "They have the backing of the Iranians." He was willing to give them the who and the what if they bought it. The when and the where was something he would hold back. They might guess, but he wouldn't tell them.

When both men were laughing at what they considered to be absurd, Bolan lurched at them, swiveling to wrench the M-16 from the guard's limp hands.

"If you make one sound, I'll empty this clip here and now." The expression on the warrior's face told the whole story.

They sat, stunned by the turn of events.

"You don't believe my story," he went on, "but that's all right. I'll have to take care of the enemy myself. If you survive, you can read about it in the papers."

14

They were losing time. Bolan gave his orders crisply.
"Patch them up and take them to Turbah's camp," he
told the doctor. "I'm going to dispose of our friends
here and I've got a call to make. I'll meet you by the
fireside."

"But my practice," the doctor said. "I'm marked
now. I'll never be able to practice again."

"Give it a few days. If everything goes as planned,
you'll be okay."

"Are you going to kill them?" Dr. Sharaf waved casually at the police, who were trussed up like turkeys
and lay in the back of the national guard truck.

"Probably not," he replied.

"I don't want bloodshed, either, but they will come
back for me?"

"Like I said, give yourself a few days. You'll be all
right."

Bolan watched the doctor pull away in a dusty Nissan. He'd join them later. Right now he had other
business to attend to. He drove the truck to a deserted
suburb of Hail and left the vehicle unattended while he
made his call.

The unlighted pay phone was near a Bedouin hotel
where most of the indigents were asleep on their reed
platforms. Recently installed electronic switching per-

mitted him to call direct with a special access code without the operator being involved. He called Brognola's private number. It was two in the morning where he was, which made it six in the evening in Washington.

"Yeah?" the familiar voice questioned from eight thousand miles away.

"Striker. We're down to the short strokes and I need your help."

"Shoot." Brognola couldn't recall ever having received so many calls from the soldier during a mission. But they had worked together long enough that the Executioner didn't need to explain himself.

Bolan knew Brognola would record the conversation, memorize the details, then wipe the tape. He raced through the details without worrying about his friend trying to scribble notes. "First you'll have to contact the new Saudi king and get amnesty for a few people." He named Turbah and his people, as well as the good doctor.

He explained the whole plan and gave Brognola the date and time. He held back only the location of the rebel encampment. "As I see it, the rebel camp has to be razed to the ground before the Saudi forces can put their plan into action."

"And you want to do it," Brognola said, beating him to the punch.

"You got it."

"And you have sufficient backup?"

"Enough."

"Okay. What else?"

"It's payback time."

"And what the hell does that mean?"

"We could strike a blow for our international image by getting back at the Soviets and Iranians."

"It would have to be something subtle," Brognola said. "Something we could leak to the foreign press. Bring me back a video of one of their people shooting off his mouth."

Bolan could hear the slurred speech and imagine the big man with an unlighted cigar rolling from side to side in his mouth as he talked. Brognola was right.

"All right. A tape. It means another trip to Umm al-Qulban. Too bad. I'd hoped that phase of the job was finished."

"If you want to put the Iranians down, I can't see any other way."

"Sure. Seems like we're backtracking, is all."

"You brought it up," the big man said. "Is that it?"

"No. I'm about to take the CID captain and his men out into the desert and turn them loose," Bolan explained. "I need someone to ride herd on them for a few days."

"How long?"

"Give me four days. It's all part of the amnesty deal, and I need some freedom to move around."

"Can do. It's not going to sit well with the Secretary of State. I'll have to go to him personally on this one."

"Whatever it takes. Get him to call the king in the next couple of hours."

IT TOOK the Executioner five hours to drive his national guard captives into the desert, unload them and get back to the camp of Turbah's people. He left his commando knife point down in the sand a hundred feet from them. He knew that with enough effort they could free themselves and get back to civilization before they

dehydrated. By that time Brognola would have someone rounding them up and keeping them occupied for
the next four days.

The Shammar camp held some pleasant surprises. It
was time for some good news for a change. Grimaldi
was in good shape and al-Murra had started to come
around. His color was good and his conversation ra-
tional.

"They are doing well," Dr. Sharaf offered. "They
are not like my patients who seem to prolong their woes.
These two seem to have a mission. It helps."

"Thanks, Doc," Bolan said. "I've talked to my
friends. They have the police in check for a few days
and will arrange an amnesty for you when this is all
over."

"I'm not sure what 'this' is. When will it be over?"
The doctor was sitting by the fire, eating food from a
tray one of the women had brought. This was the first
time Bolan had seen him at rest. He was a good-looking
man, clean-shaven, but with countless worry lines at his
eyes and mouth from too much work and too little
sleep.

"Soon. You can leave here in five days without worrying about reprisals."

"When do we take off?" Grimaldi asked.

Bolan knew that the pilot expected them to fly to
Mecca and set up their base right away. "In good time,"
he replied. "We've got another job to do first."

"What job?" Grimaldi asked.

"I've agreed to bring back proof of the dealings involving the Rashidis, Iranians and Russians."

"How the hell are we going to do that?" Grimaldi
asked. "Take pictures?"

Bolan nodded.

"I'm right, aren't I? You're going to risk your life taking some pictures so some eggheads in Washington can look them over. What the hell good is that?" Grimaldi failed to hide his annoyance.

"Don't knock it, Jack. If we can make the Soviets and the Iranians look dirty, the Soviet ties with the Syrians will be weakened. Their strength in the Middle East will be set back for years."

"So how do we get the pictures?" Adnan al-Murra spoke for the first time.

"We've got to go back to Umm al-Qulban, right?" Salman Turbah said, a gleam in his eye. "After blowing their fortress all to hell, you're going back."

"I don't like it any more than you do. We've got to capture one of the brothers. We'll make a tape of his confession and leave him for the Saudis to question later."

"You and I?" Turbah asked.

"Yeah. If you'll do it."

The young man laughed as he lunged from his place at the fire to embrace his new friend in the Saudi way, kissing him on both cheeks before Bolan could react. "I knew you'd shake up this place. I'm going to enjoy this."

THE TWO LIMOUSINES were parked on a deserted part of the tarmac at Andrews Air Force Base. In one, the driver sat alone, waiting. In the other, two men talked quietly. A partition separated them from the driver.

"I don't like this, Mr. Brognola," the Secretary of State pointed out. His face was grave in the dim light. "This is downright dangerous."

"Sorry, sir, but my man in Saudi Arabia has come through with the information we want."

"Spill it."

"Sounds like a cheap thriller. The Iranians are in it with the Soviets. They're teamed up for the first time and are using the Arab tribe as their front."

"Sounds unlikely. The Soviets are too close to the Iraqi cause for me to believe that," the powerful secretary said as if to himself. "The Soviets want the Iranians defeated," he went on. "They haven't supplied the Iraqis directly, but we have intelligence that they send in arms indirectly."

"So why not use every tool they can? If they team up with the Iranians now, they could take over Saudi with a puppet government."

"The Saudis favor a kingdom. It wouldn't be a kingdom with the Soviets behind it."

"But if an obscure prince of the family had no other way to gain power?" Brognola pressed, letting it hang there.

"It sounds too preposterous."

"My man heard it firsthand from a meeting of the Soviets with some ayatollahs. Their plan is to kidnap the king in the Harram at the start of the hajj."

"That's all we have to know," the secretary said. "I'll notify the royal family and the army will clean it up."

"I don't have the exact information," Brognola protested. "The Saudis would lose a lot of men trying to find the enemy stronghold in Mecca."

"Does your man know where it is?"

Brognola didn't want an official rebuke or a total loss of confidence in his people. "I'm sure it would be best if we let him complete his job" was all he said.

"And enter the Harram, an infidel?"

"He knows what he's doing. His presence won't be traced back to us."

"So what am I doing here in the middle of the night?" the secretary demanded.

"Don't let this get to you, sir. It seems logical to notify the Saudi royal family, but I'm sure we don't even know who to trust now. My man will take a videotape confession from one of the principals and make sure we get it."

"I still don't see why I'm here. You could have kept to the same plan for all the leeway you've left me."

"You've been connected with State for a long time, sir," Brognola said, looking at the steel-gray eyes of the man next to him. "What can you add to what I've told you? If they plan to take over the Great Mosque and capture the king, can we expect action in any other places? What should we anticipate that we don't know?"

"In the 1979 fiasco in Mecca several other pockets of Shiite resistance sprung up. They should be watched."

"Will you keep this to yourself until I get back to you?"

"What do you intend to do?"

"The Mecca attempt is under control," Brognola said, taking a wrapped cigar from his pocket and holding it in a warm hand. "I'll warn my man about possible Shiite activity elsewhere. He can be looking for it. If he confirms any activity, I'll let you know right away."

"And at that point I contact the Saudi royal family. I see."

"Sooner. I know I suggested we might be talking to the wrong party and mess this up, but what I'm suggesting is we find out who we can trust at the top before the action starts. Find out, but don't tell them why."

"All right," the secretary acquiesced. "I'll go along with this, but it better not blow up in my face."

"It won't."

"Is your man the one the President would expect you to send on a job like this?"

"The best man I know."

The secretary nodded, satisfied for the moment. He had guessed the identity of the man who was fighting their battle. The man had come through for them before. It always seemed ironic to him that such a man should be officially out in the cold when he personally knew so many thieves and traitors in Washington who were cloaked in respectability.

It would always be that way. Politics and patriotism were seldom found in the same body these days. He turned to Brognola and nodded.

The interview was over.

IN A SIMILAR MEETING two men sat in a stretch Mercedes limousine south of Riyadh at a lookout on the road to Al-Kharj. One man was dressed as a prince should be. His robe and headdress were of the finest Egyptian cotton. His dark brown cloak was made of expensive broadcloth. The gold-colored embroidery, usually of fiber, was of the finest spun gold. Prince Bandar was clean-shaven, youthful and athletic. He had been in Switzerland learning the banking business until recently. A late son of Ibn Saud, he was well down the line of ascendancy.

The other man was dressed in a business suit. His clothes weren't Eastern Bloc, but the features of the man and his pronunciation of English were. He smoked a foul-smelling cigarette without asking permission. His questions and answers were blunt and to the point.

"You are sure the Iranians have enough men to pull it off?" the prince asked nervously.

"I have reassured you many times."

"It looks like either Abdullah or Sultan will be named king tomorrow. Even now I'm not sure which."

"It doesn't matter."

"I want to be sure they are both killed. Sultan has the loyalty of the armed forces. Abdullah has controlled the national guard for so long that he thinks of them as his private bodyguard."

"They will both suffer the same fate."

"Are you sure that none of my most powerful brothers will be left alive?"

"We have discussed this before. When we have control, we will do exactly as you wish."

The prince was obviously nervous. He wouldn't be present at the actual killings, but the thought of any of his older, most powerful brothers surviving gave him nightmares. "What about the ayatollahs?" he asked. "We can't let them assume power at all. That is one condition I must insist on."

"I have told you, Excellency. The only workable plan for us is if both the Iranians and Rashidis are controlled. All you have to do is keep out of it until we come for you. Tell no one. When it is over, the Iranians, the Rashidis and your older brothers will have disappeared. Trust me."

The younger prince chewed at the sleeve of his cloak, deep in thought. "All right. I'm glad you came."

The Soviet organizer, a major in the KGB, opened the door and slipped out, surrounded by a cloud of his own cigarette smoke.

He walked to the white Buick parked fifty feet away. Before he opened the door, he flipped his cigarette onto the asphalt of the lookout and stood, taking in deep breaths of the dry night air. The lookout was at least three thousand feet above the plain and the winding road that led to Al-Kharj. The moon shone like a great beacon, bathing everything in front of him in eerie light. Several buttes thrust sandstone fingers skyward.

He opened the car door and slid in beside the driver.

"What did the young fool want this time?" the driver, a captain of the KGB, asked.

"Assurance as usual. We can't blame him. We are lucky to find a man who is so ambitious and so stupid at the same time."

"But he will live to rule the kingdom."

"He will live, Sergei, but he will not rule. He will be fed scraps while our people, his advisers, deal with the rest of the world."

"We have enough oil, comrade," the driver replied. "All we can do is keep others from getting the Saudi oil."

"Remind me to recommend you for a course in world economics, my young friend. 'All we can do'? Believe me, it is enough."

15

Turbah trudged along, dressed in the humble robes assumed by merchants, rich and poor alike, his robe and headdress no better than the poorest Rashidi. Bolan was posing as his father, an ancient who had suffered a stroke and who couldn't talk. His eyes looked dull, but they didn't miss a detail. The mission was to kidnap a Rashidi, but in the process they would pick up any intelligence they could.

The cargo their camels carried included muslins, silks, cotton prints and rolls of feathery lace. The bolts of dress material would gain him access to the tongues of women as well as men, women who had nothing better to do than sit at slatted windows, watching. Before the two men could pull off a kidnapping, they had to know the lay of the land.

The young Shammar pitched a tent outside the town as close as he could to a communal well. He cooked their meals and wasn't bothered by the Rashidis, who paid little heed to traveling merchants. Women came to the stall he set up, haggled, traded gold bangles for bolts of cloth and carried away their new treasures. They nodded to the blank face of the old man, who was the merchant's father.

Turbah watched and waited.

On the first night, as they walked through the main street, Turbah supporting his "father," the young man found a small Bedouin hotel he hadn't noticed before. The beds, framed with dried desert vines, held together with rotting cord, served only to keep the pallets of the weary from the ground. Several of the beds were pulled together in a circle as local tribesmen smoked and talked. He sat his "father" in an empty space, paid one riyal for a pipe, crossed his legs like the others and listened.

"You have not been here before, merchant," one man noted.

"It is true. I have not. I am from Jordan. I made my pilgrimage last year and stayed to roam your land."

"The old man is your father?"

"The man who sired me. Allah will take him soon," Turbah said sadly. "He does not understand much and speaks not at all."

"In the village we have the same. Better a stricken father who cannot talk than a wife who can," a near-sighted young man with thick glasses observed.

"A man without a wife is twice as lucky as the man with one," a fat man added as they all laughed.

"You have few strangers here?" Turbah asked them innocuously.

"Few. When they come at all, they come in groups," one man offered.

"And some are strange," another said. They all wanted to be part of the discussion.

"Am I so strange?" he asked.

"You? You are like us. Some come in clothes unfit for our climate and wearing strange headdresses—very strange. You should have been here for the excitement.

An American was here and blew a hole in the fortress. A lot of bodies were carted away.''

Turbah decided to go slowly. The conversation drifted to news of other tribes, the condition of the flocks, the number of moons since the last rain. Turbah's mind began to wander. Finally they talked about the hit on the fortress.

''...he vanished into the heavens as if Allah had taken him for punishment.''

''...if he vanished, he must have been standing next to my donkey, for it vanished the same day.''

The snatches of conversation registered on Turbah. ''What tale is this?'' he asked.

''Men come in helicopters. Some are dressed in strange Western clothes. Others are mullahs, ayatollahs, fiends who fuel the fires of hatred,'' an old man bent with arthritis said. ''Some were killed in the explosion, but others will come.''

''Why are they here?'' Turbah asked. ''Do they not have enough to keep them busy at home?''

''They will spread their war to our village,'' one of the men said, waving the mouthpiece of his hookah. ''They are evil men.''

''What do you think, merchant?'' a hawk-nosed villager asked.

''I am a simple merchant. It is best for me to stay clear of local politics,'' Turbah said. ''But I do wonder why the Rashid brothers would host such people. I've heard that the one, Hussein, is an able leader.''

''He is an able man but a stubborn one,'' the hawk-nosed man replied.

''He is in town now?'' Turbah asked. He had thought the eldest Rashid brother was dead.

"He is. We are not supposed to know, but he is waiting for a meeting tomorrow night. Two of the helicopters will fly in with more of Hussein's new allies. It will be a big meeting," the man with the distinctive nose said, the fire of conspiracy burning from the deep sockets of troubled eyes. "I'm told by my cousin who is a tea boy at the fortress that this is the last big meeting. He knows not what they talk of, but he heard they plan a small war of some kind."

"Where?" Turbah asked, looking shocked, playing his role to the hilt.

Bolan's expression never changed. He could understand no more than half of what they said.

"No one knows. We think it is in the kingdom."

"And you have told no one?"

They looked at him with disgust. "We are curious old men. We are not stupid old men," one answered.

Turbah had learned nothing he didn't know, except that the townspeople weren't in on the Rashidi activity. He knew Hussein was in town and a big meeting would take place the next night. Time was getting short. They had to be back at his home camp in no more than two days. "I have come from Hail. People talk of the death of another brother," he said. "It is a grievous thing."

"Unlike Ibn Saud, old Ibn Rashid did not spew out sons like a machine for cigarettes. He had only eight sons. Four are left." The remark came from an old Rashidi guard, sitting with bandoliers of ammunition over each shoulder and an ancient rifle at his side.

"These men with the heavy clothing, could they have killed the brother in Hail? It is possible," Turbah added.

"No. They came as friends. A Westerner killed Hamza, an American it is said. He was the one who came here to kill. Allah has punished him," a wizened old man croaked out.

"The strange friends come again soon," the old guard offered. "Your tea boy cousin is right."

"The man who knows all," the others chorused, laughing at him.

"It is true, I tell you. Rooms are being prepared for them now. They sleep off the floor on platforms. They are coming tomorrow or the next day."

"And the hated ayatollah? Is the Shiite leader coming also?" the wizened old man asked as he spit in the sand.

"Does one come without the other? Our Rashidi masters are mad to deal with one such as he," a young man said, speaking for the first time, his distaste apparent.

Turbah put down his pipe and climbed from the rickety bed frame. "I thank you for the friendship. I find the conversation different from the peaceful villages to the south. You men are fortunate Allah has shown you so much of life. It keeps your tongues from sticking to the roofs of your mouths."

They all laughed at his humor, so like their own. He took Bolan by the arm and trudged down the street, feet scuffing the dust, shoulders stooped to disguise his height. Turbah knew it wouldn't be long—one more day of selling goods to the women.

Turbah explained to Bolan all that had been said.

"We'll wait for the visitors," Bolan said. "We'll take Hussein captive, but we might get a crack at all of them in the process. If it doesn't stop the plan, it will slow them down."

"And what will you do?" Turbah asked.

"I'm established as a senile old man. You carry on as you would. I'll sit in front of the tent."

"Just be careful."

Turbah returned to the circle of men, smoked a ragged old hookah and exchanged jokes about other tribes and customs. He had almost forgotten that such simple tranquillity existed.

THE NEXT DAY three cars drove into town in a cloud of dust. So much for the story about helicopters. As Turbah watched, four Europeans in heavy business suits and high-crowned fedoras spilled out of the first car. Three ayatollahs and a group of others climbed from the other cars. Turbah assumed the other four were guards—eleven men in all. At the gate to the Rashidi palace three men rushed out to greet the new arrivals. One huge man was heavily bandaged. He had to be Hussein. Now the count was fourteen.

Turbah continued to sell goods to the woman for another hour. As his last customer disappeared, he packed up his wares and slowly walked to the rear of the palace, ambling up to the two guards at the rear gate and asking for a light. They were Rashidi house guards, not part of the group he'd seen earlier.

As the first guard flashed his lighter and the attention of both guards was on the flame, a razor-sharp knife appeared in Turbah's hand. As he slit the throat of the first man, the second guard swung his rifle around, his finger caressing the trigger. Suddenly he collapsed to the ground, blood rushing from the horrible slash across his throat.

"You were about to start without me?" Bolan asked, bending to wipe the stained commando knife on the guard's robe.

"No. I read you well. You were about ten seconds earlier than I told myself."

The rear gate faced the mountain, so they hadn't been observed. They dragged the two guards inside the compound and hid their bodies behind a dilapidated truck.

They removed their sandals and proceeded through the unguarded back door, the tile cool beneath their feet. They could sense movement nearby, and the scent of roasting meat wafted from the kitchen.

Turbah rounded the first corner cautiously. A guard from the cars lounged against a wall. He had his back to them, smoking. The silenced Beretta coughed discreetly, and the guard dropped almost as quietly. They carried the man to a food locker and wiped up the trail of blood.

Bolan turned the next corner and spotted another guard. The startled man opened his mouth to shout an alarm, clawing for his holstered automatic. Turbah rushed forward, chopped at his throat, crushing small bones against the man's windpipe. The guard died with his hands clasping his throat, his tongue protruding, struggling for air.

A stairway to their right was the route the group had taken. They heard female voices on the first floor, male voices on the upper level. Bolan disliked the layout. He always felt vulnerable on stairs, vulnerable from two directions. But this time he had a man at his back.

They made their way to the second floor, pausing at the doorway of a room at the top of the stairs where two Rashidi guards sat talking. Turbah slipped inside the room, greeting them formally. Taking advantage of the men's surprise, he rushed at one guard, taking him out with one upward thrust of his curved blade, choking off an alarm from lungs filling with blood. Bolan slashed the blade of his commando knife across the throat of the other guard.

Turbah searched the room quietly, looking for weapons. At the bottom of a box of discarded wrappings he found three American antipersonnel grenades. He handed two to Bolan and kept one for himself.

The next three rooms were empty. As they eased their heads around a corner, they saw the last two guards outside a closed door. They could hear voices raised in anger.

The corridor leading to the voices was long and narrow, a twin to the wing that had been destroyed in Bolan's previous raid. They couldn't get to the guards without alarming those in the room. The men were Arabs, probably with the ayatollahs—Iranians in Western dress carrying compact Russian automatic weapons. They might respond to some distractions that intensely trained KGB men would not. The two warriors retreated to the first floor, confident they had disposed of all opposition there.

Bolan had a plan, but he knew it wouldn't be easy. He whispered in Turbah's ear. It might be a long shot, but they had few alternatives.

The least risky would involve the women of the household. Bolan lifted the body of the dead guard from the food locker and threw it into the kitchen among the women. As they screamed, he moved to the bottom of the stairs, hoping their cries would draw the guards.

They did—he could hear the men pounding down the stairs. Would he be right about the rest—or lucky?

At the bottom Bolan slugged the first guard in the gut as he passed. The second man tripped over the first.

Neither moved. The women were still screaming. Would the men upstairs hear them over their heated debate?

The women had fled outside, and it wouldn't be long before the village would be roused. For now, time was on their side. Whoever said a good offense was the best defense knew what he was talking about. If they could maintain the offensive, they would keep a step ahead.

No one stirred upstairs. Bolan ripped a Russian subgun from one of the unconscious guards, climbed the steps two at a time and moved swiftly to the door. He listened. The language was English. Someone, an ayatollah, translated for the Russians.

It was a repetition of what they had heard before from men who were now dead. Bolan had heard enough. He was tempted to hear more—to learn if there was more, but Turbah was attacking from another angle and timing was essential. And he could hear noise below even if those in the room were unaware of it.

"If Iran is to control the Gulf—"

He crashed through the door and burst into the room. Eleven faces turned to him in alarmed surprise. Hands reached for weapons as Bolan brought up the purloined Russian piece and sprayed the room. Turbah entered the window from a balcony, clubbed Hussein and had him halfway out the window before the man could react.

Hussein turned and slashed at his attacker. Turbah retaliated, intending to inflict only a minor wound, but his knife cut too deeply, and the big man sank to his knees, blood pouring from his chest in a crimson stream.

A smaller version of the eldest Rashid rushed to the prone figure, screaming out his grief. Turbah grabbed the small man and disappeared out the window. The whole action had taken less than half a minute.

Bolan pulled the pin on a grenade, and as he ducked into the hallway, he flung it into a far corner where most of the occupants had fled. The roar of the exploding device assaulted his ears as he curled himself in a ball next to the recently replaced doorframe, out of range. A wave of pressure flung the battered door off its hinges, debris and human flesh following close behind.

It seemed like minutes, but it was only seconds before Bolan poked his head through the doorway to view the carnage. Screams and low moans filled the room. Blood was everywhere. At the far end, possible thirty feet away, someone tried to rise. Bolan pulled a second pin and lobbed the grenade among the ruins. Again he ducked for what protection he could find.

To sensitive ears the second explosion seemed louder than the first. This time no one moved as he peered around the shattered frame. No one moved and no one moaned.

Feet pounded on the stairs. Bolan had to move. He didn't know how many rounds were left in the Russian weapon in his hand. He still had the Beretta. As he considered his situation, he stepped across the pile of dead to a rear window. The explosions had blown it outward, cleaning all glass from the frame.

He looked out. Turbah had the small Rashid on the ground and was waiting. The three white limousines were still out front. It seemed quiet. Instead of running out to see what had happened, the townspeople were cowering inside their homes. As he prepared to jump to freedom, Bolan heard women screaming for help behind him.

They were screaming in English.

He turned to the far door and listened. They were two doors down the halls. He was sure he'd checked all the rooms, and if he hadn't heard the voices before, when he was a captive, he wouldn't have believed his ears.

Bolan ran back down the hall and smashed in the door with the butt of his rifle. Three women huddled in a corner, their skirts bunched around their thighs, their hands and feet bound by hemp.

He slashed the ropes with his commando knife. They started to thank him, crying, asking questions. He cut them short. They had no time to lose. "We've got to get out of here—now. Can you walk?" he asked.

The women were filthy, their clothes in tatters, their hair like rats' nests. They struggled to their feet, weak and stiff, but they could walk. He charged down the stairs ahead of them. As they stumbled after him, he encountered the two guards he had knocked out. They were starting to grope with furniture, trying to rise. Bolan had no time for niceties. As the women appeared on the scene, round-eyed, he shot each man in the head.

"Wait here until I shout for you."

He looked around the doorjamb. No one was in sight. Turbah was covering him. As he moved he heard something click. He whirled and fired at a guard coming around the side of the house. As the guard went down, a hole in his neck, Turbah whirled to cover the Executioner's back with an AK he had picked up. A second guard raised his automatic weapon. Turbah's AK spewed out hot tumblers and the man went down. The small Rashidi brother squatted on the ground, clinging to the bottom of Turbah's robe, whimpering.

Bolan crept to the edge of the palace and looked around the corner. No guards—no people—nothing.

He checked the other side—nothing. Picking up an AK-47 rifle Turbah had missed, he threw it onto the front seat of the lead vehicle and shouted to the women. By the time they had stumbled out and stood waiting by the car, he had circled the compound and shot out the tires of all the vehicles he could see.

"Who are the women? Where did they come from?" Turbah asked.

"Don't know. They were captives, so we've got company. Get in the back and keep your heads down," he ordered the women. "Throw the prisoner in back with them. I'm heading for Hail," he told Turbah. "Sit on him," he said to the women. "I need him as evidence later."

He jumped behind the wheel again, the engine roaring under the weight of his heavy foot. As he circled the compound, Bolan directed, "Shoot the wheels off everything you see, but try to conserve ammunition."

As they careered around the compound and out into the open, the Kalashnikov chattered and 7.62 mm slugs tore holes in the tires of cars and trucks parked at random in the compound. Several hot tumblers hit gas tanks, and the explosions sent up clouds of black smoke billowing over orange and red clusters of flame. The smoke followed that of the earlier blast into the sky and the westward drift. It probably could be seen from Hail by now.

THE ROAD CURVED to the east and then southeast as Bolan urged the white Buick along the dusty rut that was the desert road to Hail, which he estimated to be about forty miles away. At the speed they were going they'd be there in less than an hour.

Hail meant safety and the protection of Turbah's people. Occasionally he looked in his rearview mirror for pursuers, but saw none. He was heading more south-southeast now, south of the Jabal Aja Hills and into the hardpan that made such excellent desert roads. If he could stay away from unmarked wadis, the ever-present dry gulches, he would make Hail with ease.

In the seat beside him, Turbah shouted with exhilaration like a kid. "We did it! Damned if we didn't do it!"

Bolan could understand the reaction. The young Shammar probably hadn't seen much action lately. He'd been as cool in battle as a veteran. He deserved to feel proud.

Suddenly a fishtail of dust was closing in on their left. Where had it come from? Either someone had radioed ahead for help or the new enemy had a shortcut.

The "how" didn't matter—he had pursuers, and they were determined. A second dust cloud appeared on their right, slightly ahead and closing.

The vehicle to his right was a Toyota four-wheel-drive. Two men were bouncing around in it, one driving and one pointing a rifle. Bolan swerved to the left. As they followed, he tried to swing back to catch them off guard. The vehicles came together before he expected, and despite the hail of lead from Turbah's AK, they got the worst of it.

The second vehicle was a Nissan pickup. As the Buick glanced off the Toyota, the pickup crushed Bolan's left fender into a tire, and he was slowed as rubber screamed on steel.

There was no way he would fight this way. If he let them get the upper hand in their own territory, he was finished. He drove with his left hand, the tortured tire screaming and churning out foul smoke. The Beretta was in his lap, fully loaded. He reached into Turbah's pocket, retrieved the last grenade, pulled the pin and held down the spring clip. It was the best offense he could devise.

They came at him again full throttle. Even with Turbah trying to spray them, Bolan felt like a sitting duck. He could see white teeth grin at him from brown faces—grins of confidence and derision. With little chance of accuracy, he pitched the grenade at the Toyota and turned his attention to the Nissan. He heard the explosion but could hear the Toyota still coming on. Damn!

Bolan picked up the Beretta as the grinning faces in the Nissan closed in. The features blurred in a mist of blood and gore as he shot both men point-blank in the face. The grins slowly disappeared as muscles went slack. It all seemed to be happening slowly...the grenade...the explosion...the grinning faces turning, relaxing into death's heads. The Nissan kept barreling straight ahead, the dead man's foot pressed on the pedal for all time.

The other vehicle was behind him and closing fast. Turbah's AK had jammed. The other SMG was on the floor in the back with the women. If he couldn't get them with the Beretta, it was all over.

The vehicle overtook him, but didn't attempt to crowd him. Were they playing games? They knew one wheel was crippled, and they were moving in for the kill. He had to come up with something fast.

They came up on his left, sitting ramrod straight, looking neither right nor left. As he raised the Beretta, he hesitated. Something was wrong. They weren't looking at him. As they passed, he could see blood-soaked shirts. He had missed the vehicle with the grenade, but shrapnel had caught up with the Arabs.

The Toyota began to slow. The driver tumbled to this left and off the seat, hitting the hardpan. Then the vehicle coasted almost to a stop. Bolan caught up with it and eased the Buick in front to the sound of screeching metal.

He told Turbah to stay with the women, pulled himself from the damaged car and ran to the 4x4. It was relatively unharmed. He put it in neutral.

The second man was dead. Bolan jerked him from the right seat and tossed him into the back of the Buick. He took a better look at the Toyota—no real damage, plenty of gas, no leaks anywhere. Good. Their lives might depend on it. He scanned the superheated desert floor for the Nissan. A line of dust was settling off to the west about three miles. The death vehicle was still rolling.

Perhaps they would stop when they hit a butte or dropped into a deep wadi. They might not be found for weeks.

The Executioner loaded in his people and turned the Toyota toward Hail.

16

Ahmed Noor Turbah stood in front of the tents, watching a cloud of dust approach from the southeast. At a hundred yards a grime-encrusted Toyota 4x4 emerged from the cloud, a battered remnant of hard times. The careering vehicle was overloaded with people, at least six or seven. The patriarch of the Turbah family recognized Bolan and Salman, his son. They were expected. From a hundred feet away the others looked like women in Western garb, their hair askew, their clothes in tatters. He guessed what had happened. To the shame of local tribes, the Rashidis had taken Western women captive before. The old man called for his women to help.

Before the Toyota came to a stop a backwash of dust covered everything within fifty feet. Grimaldi stood beside the old man while Dr. Sharaf hurried from a tent.

"This one's a Rashid?" Grimaldi asked as Bolan pulled their prisoner from the Toyota.

"Best we could do," Bolan said. "Hussein survived our first probe but not this one."

"You sure this one knows the whole plan?" Grimaldi asked. "He doesn't look like my idea of a warrior."

Salman Turbah jumped from the Toyota and embraced his father. The two men exchanged kisses, two to the left cheek and one to the right. "We have some females who need help," he said when he released the old man.

"I've sent for our women. It appears that the Rashidis have been up to their old tricks again. Where did you find them?"

"Ford found them tied up and living in filth in an upstairs room. They had been used badly."

Both men left the accusations unspoken. The Rashidis were decimated. The sad-looking character they had brought back was probably the last of old Ibn Rashid's progeny.

"I'd like a tent erected away from the others," Bolan said, addressing himself to the head of the family.

"We have one." He pointed to the far end of the encampment where a lone goatskin tent stood empty. "Use it as you will."

"Come on, Doc," Bolan said to Sharaf. Then he turned to Grimaldi, who was helping the women out of the Toyota. "Bring your small leather case. And the videocamera Brognola sent."

Bolan had the short, chubby Rashid by the arm and was dragging him toward the isolated tent. Sharaf trailed behind, uncertain of his role. Grimaldi disappeared for a moment to reappear with both the leather case and the camera juggled in his one good hand.

"What's this all about?" Sharaf asked as Bolan deposited the terrified Rashid on the rug inside the tent flap.

"We know most of the Rashidi plan," Bolan told him. "I need to know all of it. We don't want to be surprised when we're taking on their whole force in Mecca."

"Mecca? You can't enter the holy city!"

Bolan looked at the man and tried to gauge his meaning. He had spent a great deal of his life in Western society. "Would you rather have the Shiites capture and kill your king, or would you turn your back and let me stop it in the holy city?"

"Stop it, of course," Sharaf said. "But if you're caught, an infidel inside the city, it doesn't matter whether you've saved the whole kingdom from the forces of evil, the ulema will have your legs. When an infidel enters the holy city, he has committed a grievous sin. The legs that took him there are forfeit. That's their law and they won't bend."

"I'm glad to see reason," Bolan said. "I'll take my chances on the justice of the holy men." He took the case from Grimaldi, took him to get the camera rolling and handed the case of drugs to Sharaf. "The red vial is a drug like scopolamine. You can handle the syringe better than anyone."

"Please. Don't use the drug. It will kill me," their prisoner begged in a quavering falsetto. "I know what they can do. Please," he continued in passable English. "I'll tell you what I know."

"Who are you?" Bolan asked, waving the doctor off. Sharaf sat in a corner of the tent and listened. Grimaldi stood near the flap of the tent where he'd have the best angle for the camera. He kept it centered on the small man, making sure no other faces appeared before the lens. Bolan sat cross-legged opposite their young captive, trying not to look menacing. Maybe this would be easy for once.

"I am Mahad ibn-Abdul Rachman Ibn-Rashid," the man said. He was shivering with fear. Sweat poured down his face from his soiled *guttra*, making the perfume he wore smell bitter.

"Are you the last of the Rashids?" Bolan asked.

"My remaining brothers were all in the room you destroyed," the man sobbed. He was a regular butterball. His round cheeks were pink and streaked with tears. His teeth were small and perfectly formed. He was more like a plump girl than one of the infamous Rashid brothers.

"If he's the last, isn't this over?" Grimaldi asked, keeping the camera and the microphone trained on the adversaries on the rug.

"The Rashidis were pawns, convenient enemies of the Saudis. This whole mess could be pinned on them," Bolan said. "The Shiites are the real enemies. And they'll be more determined than ever since we killed off some of their top people." Bolan let the small man settle down. He seemed to relax a little, the fear that was evident abating as he saw he wasn't going to be harmed. After a moment or two during which Turbah's tea boy arrived, filled cups of steaming tea for them and left, Bolan related what they knew about the Shiite plan. "What can you tell us that we don't know?" he concluded. "And remember that we have the drugs if you don't tell all you know." He leaned closer, his face just a few inches from Mahad's. The camera was zoomed in to exclude Bolan's features. "And we can use force. How much pain can you stand?" he asked.

The effect was startling. "You probably don't have the Mecca address," Mahad blurted out. "Everything you've said is correct. It is a large compound with a pink wall around it. The top of the wall is green. We don't have house numbers in Mecca, but it is at the corner of King Faisal and Hafayir streets."

"That's near the northwest corner of the Harram," Bolan finished for him. "How far is that from the Great Mosque?"

"Maybe fifteen kilometers. It would take less than a half hour by truck to drive to the mosque."

"You have been to this compound?" Bolan asked.

"Yes. I helped to rent it."

"What else is at the corner of King Faisal and Hafayir?" Bolan asked. The others stayed out of the conversation.

Mahad picked up the tea and took a few sips of the steaming liquid. He sighed, resigned to his fate. The fear had left his face, softening it, bringing out the feminine features with more clarity than ever.

"Apartments for the pilgrims."

"How tall are they?"

"Tall? What means 'tall'?"

"How many floors? Are they very big, or are they small?"

The small man thought about it for a moment, then closed his eyes as if conjuring up the scene in his mind. "They are not all the same. Some are three stories. Some are four or five. None are very tall."

"Okay. If you continue to help, you'll eventually be set free. If we find that you're lying, we'll turn you over to the royal family," he went on, staring hard at Mahad. "Go ahead. What else?"

Bolan evaluated the man as he spoke. The threat had no effect on him. He decided the small man was telling them the straight goods.

"What do you want to know?" Mahad asked.

"Does the national guard have an armory close to the compound?"

Mahad seemed surprised. "Yes," he said. "In the Al-Zahra district just to the south, about four kilometers."

Bolan digested the information. It was important. "Are the Shiites planning anything else?" he asked, throwing out the random question while he thought about the armory and what it meant to him.

"They have four strongholds spread throughout the kingdom that will rise up. The same ones that gave the Saudis trouble in 1979."

"What's he talking about?" Bolan asked Turbah. This was something new, something unexpected.

"Some areas in the kingdom still have a predominantly Shiite population," Salman said. "When they are peaceful, the royal family leaves them alone."

"Where are they?" Bolan asked.

"Abqaiq in the east is the most dangerous. It's in the middle of our oil fields. Jaizan in the south is the most militant," Turbah recalled. "Al-Hadithah in the north is close to the Iraq border, doorway to invasion from the north. Badr on the Red Sea coast is the fourth. It is a seaport that could be big trouble some day."

"How many men could they muster?" Bolan asked.

"Not a real army," Turbah said. "Maybe five hundred equipped with new SMGs."

Bolan made a mental note of the facts for reporting to Brognola. He couldn't tackle them all. They should be hit all at once by four separate, superior forces while he was tackling the Mecca layout.

Bolan had enough to think about and more problems than he could handle. He was sure Mahad had told him the truth and wasn't holding back. Did he know anything else? He put the question to the small man.

"No," Mahad said, then spouted off a tirade of justification for Rashidi actions based on ideals that meant nothing to Bolan. The Executioner waited for the man to calm down, then took him through all the details again, making sure they agreed with the first telling. He signaled for Grimaldi to stop filming.

"You'll come to Mecca with us. If we're successful, we'll recommend clemency for you. If we fail..."

He was about to get up and leave them to walk under the stars and do some heavy thinking when a final question hit him. Then another. "How well do you know the coast around Mecca?" he asked.

"Like my home. I worked for the government in their summer headquarters in Taif."

"Does any of the coastline need pesticide spraying from the air?"

The small man thought about it. "I remember a small spraying camp off the Christian Road between Taif and Jidda."

"How far from Mecca?"

"Twenty-five kilometers. Maybe twenty. Maybe thirty."

That would be between fourteen and twenty miles, Bolan thought. "What about Saudi air defense in that area? Do you know anything about it?"

"They have none right there," Mahad said, finishing the last of his tea.

"Then where would they defend Mecca from?" Bolan asked.

Mahad hesitated to answer a question about military location but apparently decided not to hold back. "Khamis Mushait in the south, Hail in the north, Al-Kharj in the east."

"Which is closest?" the Executioner asked, making sure he had everything he could before he went into action.

"Khamis Mashait is the closest and the largest, maybe four hundred kilometers away."

Two hundred and fifty miles, Bolan told himself. They could have fighters in the area within a few minutes.

BOLAN COULD FEEL the adrenaline rush as they pulled up to where they had hidden the Cessna. This was the real beginning of his war in Saudi Arabia. Everything preceding this action had been intelligence work.

The Cessna looked exactly as they had left it. Grimaldi wasn't in as good shape, but he could fly with one hand. Bolan sometimes felt his friend could fly something like this blindfolded.

Turbah was as anxious as a puppy with a bone held only inches from its nose. Al-Murra had recovered miraculously and was calmer, more thoughtful, his attitude like that of a veteran on the eve of battle. Mahad Rashid was cowed, growing more afraid as they drew closer to the climax.

They had left the elder Turbah two hours earlier in convoy with the truck that was taking the women to Riyadh and their embassies. The older Turbah had grinned at them bravely, shook hands all around and hugged his son, knowing they were going to face odds of fifty or more to one.

They had parted from the other truck a few miles south of camp and skirted Hail well to the south before heading for the hills to the north and the hidden aircraft.

The revving of the plane's engine brought Bolan out of his reverie. They taxied for only fifty feet before the oversized wings of the Cessna gave them lift. Grimaldi followed the hills to the southeast, keeping the aircraft below a hundred feet. The air base and its radar was on the other side of the hills a few miles north of the Shammar camp they had just left.

It was the same all the way to Mecca. They flew over the semidesert, keeping the highway from Buraida to Medina in view, then cut across it when they saw no traffic, and headed for Taif and the mountains.

The summer capital was their greatest risk. It was perched on a range of mountains and overlooked the coastal plain. Since the whole council of ministers and most of the royal family lived there in the summer, the city was ringed by several radar installations.

Grimaldi picked up the Sarawat Mountains at Al-Madiq, north of Taif, and followed the range almost to the summer capital, weaving in and out of the treacherous peaks, not giving the radar anything to get a fix on.

Just before they got to the mountain road below Taif where the king and his brothers had been killed, Grimaldi banked sharply to the right and took them down eight thousand feet to the coastal plain, not crossing a major highway until he saw the turnoff where the Christian Road led unbelievers away from the holy city.

"Where's the pesticide camp?" he asked Mahad.

The small man took his head out of an airsickness bag and looked out the window, which was tinted light green. It added to the effect of the wretch's sickness. "To the left, maybe another ten kilometers," he said.

Grimaldi brought the plane out of its smooth dive and skimmed the scruff pine of the semidesert, spooking herds of Brahma bulls and multicolored goats. All the houses were made of stone but looked deserted. A stream, the first Bolan had seen in the country, ran a crooked path through a green valley. In the distance they could see a long, flat area marked by aircraft wheels. It was a remote site well away from highways and people.

Grimaldi brought the Cessna down in a perfect three-point landing. Bolan couldn't help but think about his first experience in the kingdom with Connors's body and the vultures. An old Cessna sat next to a huge storage area of metal drums. Two men with huge potbellies, looking like anything but the pilots they probably were, waved them down, huge grins splitting their faces.

When Bolan and his men taxied to the second aircraft and climbed down, the two fat men greeted them in Italian and waved a bottle of Chianti in invitation. Hoping that the men would be amenable to making a few extra bucks, the warrior walked over to them to secure parking space for the Cessna and the loan of a truck.

THEY ENTERED MECCA from the junction of the Christian Road and Pilgrim Way. The highway led to Al-Risiyfah Road, Hafayir Street and to the Great Mosque.

They had time to look the city over. The Italians had gladly lent them an excellent Land Rover. From its windows they could see the city's towering minarets. The sight was breathtaking. It had to humble new pilgrims who already believed in the one true god and his strength. To a nonbeliever the mosque was still awesome, huge, several city blocks long and as many wide. Bolan had been educated on some of the ceremony.

Several times during the ten days of the hajj as many as two million Muslims entered the mosque at the same time to circle the Holy Kabah. Now he could see that it was possible.

Turbah was driving with Grimaldi beside him. Bolan was in back with Mahad between him and al-Murra. They couldn't take any chances with the man. He seemed to have gained confidence since they'd left the Italians, as if he expected some kind of dramatic rescue. Bolan had warned his companions to watch for any kind of break.

"Where's the Shiite compound?" Bolan asked Mahad.

"Left. Maybe twelve kilometers. Maybe fifteen."

"The odometer is in kilometers," Grimaldi offered.

"Find King Faisal Street and we'll follow it west," Bolan told Turbah.

They traveled for less than half an hour when they came to the intersection. Many of the men they saw were dressed in their hajj clothing. The garment looked like three white terry-cloth towels sewn together to form a three-quarter-length robe. The men were bare-headed, many with their heads shaved.

"Why do they shave their heads?" Grimaldi asked Turbah.

"It is not part of the ritual. Many men do not comb their hair. When they remove their *guttra*, their hair looks wild."

"Dead man's hair," Bolan offered.

"Some call it that," Turbah said, concentrating on his driving, turning onto Hafayir Street and pulling over.

The women they saw were all veiled. Here, unlike Riyadh, the variety of the veils was almost endless.

Some women wore metal ones made of gold mesh adorned with gold coins. Other masks were fashioned with several kinds of metal, some precious and others copper or brass. Most of the women colored their hands in varying hues as if to attract attention to their femininity by decorating the only human flesh they were allowed to show.

"Drive around the block," Bolan said.

The wall was pink with a green stripe around the top as Mahad had told them. It took up a whole city block on each side. They couldn't see inside, but as they passed a huge open gate, several buildings were visible.

"Stop here," Bolan ordered. He turned to al-Murra. "I want you to look over every building around the compound. You know what to look for. Pick up something to write on and make a sketch of the whole area. We'll be back at this spot in one hour."

"Where are you heading?" al-Murra asked as he climbed out of the Land Rover.

"Is that what they taught you in the SAS?" Bolan asked, his face expressionless.

"No. I take orders. But I know the city a little. I thought I could help."

"We've got our guide right here," he said, taking the Beretta from his robe and hiding it between himself and Mahad. "We're going to look over the armory and I'm going to call my base," the Executioner told him. "Be here in an hour. I don't want to be spotted circling the block."

As they left al-Murra and headed for a small store on the opposite side of the street, Bolan decided to call Brognola before he went to the armory. They found a row of pay phones in the next block in front of a huge hostel for single pilgrims.

In Washington Brognola picked up the phone as if he had been waiting for the call.

"The videotape is being delivered to our embassy in Riyadh," Bolan told him. "We're in Mecca and have done a preliminary recon. We can destroy our objective without casualties."

"You got a back door?"

"All set up."

"Where you heading?" Brognola asked.

"Look for us where I picked up the Cessna."

"Will do. When?"

"If all goes well, we'll hit tomorrow at first light. But I've got something new for you." He repeated the information Mahad had told him about the other Shiite strongholds.

"The men from State suspected as much. What's your recommendation?"

"It's a problem. If we tell the Saudi military now, they'll suspect that Mecca is being hit also. They'll screw up my plan."

"So what do you want me to do?"

"The king is to make his obeisance, to scrub the floor of the Kabah tomorrow at noon. The other rebels probably plan to start their uprisings at about noon to coincide with the one in Mecca." He paused for a moment to let it sink in, then he remembered Brognola would be taping it. "Why don't you inform the military at eight? They'll have heard about our show by then and they'll be on an alert. If they can't get to the rebel camps in strength by noon, they shouldn't be in the business."

"One last thing," Brognola said. "You have to keep a low profile on this, remember?"

"I'm not going to wave the flag, but I have two Saudis on my team. They won't keep the lid on it after we're gone. There's no way I can stop that."

Brognola was silent for a few seconds. "Okay. Nothing you can do about that. Our people will deny it, but the Soviets and the Iranians will know it's true. I like it. Maybe it will send a message to people like Khaddafi and Nidal."

"What about the amnesty for my people here?"

"All set. You can tell them to lie low for a few days and the heat will be off."

"What about the police captain?"

Brognola was silent for a few seconds.

"Don't tell me," Bolan said.

"Sorry, pal. All you can hope for is to get it done and get the hell out."

"With both the military and the national guard on my tail."

"Anything else?"

"That's it," he replied. "We have to come up with some hardware and we're all set. Should be about fourteen hours, give or take."

"Good luck."

17

They had a hell of a lot to do and very little time to do it. But they had to have a home base, and to find one the day before the commencement of the hajj was impossible.

"Any ideas?" Bolan asked.

"Give me a few minutes on the phone," al-Murra replied.

The fifteen minutes before he came back were tense. They sat in the Land Rover, exposed, with hundreds of thousands of Muslims passing by and with Mahad obviously desperate to get their attention.

Al-Murra returned with a grin on his face. "An uncle lives near here. He has an unoccupied house in his compound."

"It's not in use during the hajj?" Turbah asked.

"He is a wealthy man. He had no desire to rent."

"Will we have enough privacy to come and go?" Bolan asked. He had no desire to share his plan with a stranger.

"You met my father," al-Murra said. "My uncle is a patriot, fiercely loyal to the royal family."

"I don't want you telling him what we plan," Bolan warned.

"I'll only tell him what he needs to know," al-Murra answered. "We can come and go, night and day. I'll explain it to him when it's over."

"Let's get started. Where is this place?" the Executioner asked.

"Al-Mansur Street. My guess is that it's less than two kilometers from the Shiite compound."

"You have the sketch I asked for?" Bolan asked as they pulled away.

"I've got it."

LESS THAN TWO HOURS later Bolan stood in the al-Murra compound, dressed in a makeshift blacksuit provided by the al-Murra women.

"I'll need some sort of black makeup for my hands and face," the Executioner explained. They already knew he planned a one-man raid on the national guard armory.

"They are doubly cautious during the hajj," Turbah warned.

"That's why you'll have to create a diversion," Bolan told him.

"A diversion?" al-Murra asked. "What do you have in mind?"

"Fire off a burst from an SMG a couple of blocks to the north of the armory. Grimaldi will do the same in another location, maybe to the south."

"I'd like to make a suggestion," al-Murra offered. "But I don't want to make you mad. Will you listen?"

"I'll listen."

"Grimaldi's wounded and he can't speak the language. He'll be on foot and a lot of things could go wrong. We need him tomorrow to fly." He hesitated for a moment, letting the suspense build. "My uncle doesn't have to know our whole plan, but he's got many loyal retainers who will do his bidding. They can create a lot of diversions, and we won't be at risk.''

Bolan thought about it for all of ten seconds. ''Sounds like a good plan. You can drive for me. Turbah can be a lookout.''

Al-Murra smiled in satisfaction. He was obviously pleased to play an important role in the plan. It was a tale he would be proud to tell at campfires for years to come.

''Check your watches,'' Bolan told them. ''I've got 11:31. At exactly two in the morning I'll hit the armory. I want the diversions to begin ten minutes before that,'' Bolan said. ''Is that clear?''

''The diversions will start at ten minutes to two,'' al-Murra repeated. ''Do you want any special weapons for the job? I'm sure my uncle can provide some.''

''Thanks, Adnan, but I don't intend to fire a shot if I can avoid it.''

''What will you use?'' al-Murra asked, confused. ''What if some men are left behind to guard the arms?''

''Leave that to me.''

THE ARMORY WAS LIT with spotlights all around the perimeter. Fortunately for the hitters a residential neighborhood had grown up around it so that the armory wasn't surrounded by an electronic moat, which it would have had in a more remote area. Turbah dropped Bolan off a block away in the shadows of a compound fence, then parked not far from the main entrance.

The man in black had his Beretta in a holster under his left armpit. A commando knife was in a sheath strapped to his right leg. The most important weapon he carried was a blackjack he'd made from soft leather and a few dozen small ball bearings the women had supplied. The blackjack, a real head knocker, was held in his right hand and attached to his wrist by a leather thong. He'd wrapped a length of thin polyethylene rope around his waist.

The front entrance, bathed in light, was manned by national guardsmen with submachine guns at the ready. Bolan climbed to a roof at the back of the building, the closest point to the armory roof. He tossed the rope across the gap. The three-pronged scaling hook he had devised caught and held on the second try.

Bolan tied the rope to a roof air-conditioning unit and looked over the scene carefully. The floodlights didn't illuminate the roof, but they came close. If he made the crossing hand over hand, his feet would be seen. He would have to hook his heels to the rope and pull himself over a foot at a time. It wasn't a prospect he relished, but it was the only way to go. As he started across, all hell broke loose in every direction for blocks around the building.

It was ten minutes to two.

While trucks took off from the armory, loaded with troops, Bolan made a superhuman hand-over-hand effort and was on the roof of the building in seconds.

The roof was deserted and dark. It was filled with strange dark objects: air conditioners, fan hoods, weird antennae, strings of wires that threatened to decapitate him if he moved too fast. One dark object was a small entranceway, which opened at his touch. He shone a faint light down the square tube that seemed to go on forever. It was the only way down, a three-foot-square perpendicular shaft with a metal ladder attached to one side.

Bolan listened for a few seconds. He could hear the odd shout in Arabic, but none of the noise seemed to be coming from the bottom of the shaft.

He made it down the ladder in five seconds, taking the rungs two at a time. He dropped to the floor and stood, pressing himself against the wall. It was an upper floor, built like a mezzanine. The armory was huge, open through the first floor. The mezzanine was obviously for the observation of ceremonies. It also contained cubicles around the outer rim, probably offices.

The place he wanted would be in a locked room somewhere at the back. Stairs led to the ground floor from each side of the mezzanine, and he took them one at a time, watching and listening every step of the way. He hadn't expected to get this far without confrontation.

Strangely, while the outside was bright with lights, the inside was not. Bolan blended with the shadows.

A light glowed in an office on the far side of the armory. Bolan kept to the shadows as he skirted the armory along the walls under the mezzanine. He could see where truck tires had burned rubber getting out of there a few minutes earlier. He could smell the rubber and the exhaust fumes. Like most armories, the place wasn't very well ventilated.

As he closed in on the office, he crouched below window level. An Arab officer was shouting into a phone and waving his arms. The phone cable ran down the wall next to Bolan. He hacked it in two with his commando knife and waited for the cursing to stop. Then he made it through the door and to the desk in three strides, swinging the blackjack, catching the Saudi officer on the left temple. The man went down. The Executioner knew the blow hadn't been too hard. He intended to lay out as few bodies as possible if everything went well. With as much speed as he could manage and still maintain silence, he pulled the unconscious man back to his chair and propped him up.

A set of keys lay in a plastic box in the top right-hand drawer of the desk. Bolan retrieved them and crept out to the open area again. In the shadows he watched the officer of the day march a squad of guards to their posts and march the quartet of off-duty men back to their barracks. That meant they had two men out front, two in back, and the others in a room where they probably couldn't hear him if he was careful.

So where were the weapons he needed? All the rooms were identified by red printing, but in Arabic. He didn't want to have to try every key in every lock. It was possible that the munitions room would be the last one he tried.

He skirted the walls under the mezzanine to the back of the building, where he found a room with barred windows. Was it the brig or the one he wanted? He tried several keys before he got the right one. The smell of urine and feces hit him full in the face as soon as he opened the door. No one had cleaned the toilets of the three small cells inside. Wrong choice.

He checked his watch. He'd been inside for ten minutes. It would have taken the troops ten minutes to reach the disturbances, another ten or so milling around asking questions, and maybe another ten to rush back. He could count on fifteen minutes at the most.

A door close to the brig had bigger lettering than any other door. Bolan tried the keys and was soon in a small room that was loaded with armament along three walls. Jackpot. Mortars would be his principal weapons. He loaded three of them onto a small motorized cart, and with great effort added a case of shells.

One wall was piled with crates of small arms. He helped himself to three M-16s and a case of ammunition, but he wanted something heavier. He found crates of 60 mm machine guns and took three of them. The ammunition was belt-loading and the crates were heavier than the mortar shells, making him wish he had brought someone with him.

Bolan caught sight of what he thought was a timer sticking out of a box. It was a radio-controlled detonator. He took a half-dozen detonators, a master control servomechanism and ten or twelve pounds of plastic explosives that looked like C-4.

Lastly he hoisted a box of fragmentation grenades into the cart. Then closing the door to block off all sound, he started the small vehicle. It was electric and made almost no noise.

So far so good. He had to get past the two guards at the front entrance and transfer the goods to the Land Rover.

As he opened the door and tooled the cart to the massive front entrance, he drew his Beretta with his right hand. He didn't want to kill the guards, but if he had no other choice, it would be them rather than him.

He was two hundred feet away from the front door when a guard suddenly swung toward him, his M-16 leveled. Bolan's shot tagged him in the right shoulder, the force of the 9 mm slug swinging him around. Steering the awkward little machine with his left hand, Bolan confronted the second guard. The Arab got off a short burst that was wild by only inches. Bolan's return fire punched the man backward, knocking him to the floor and sending the M-16 flying.

The barracks door burst open and a half-dozen guardsmen poured out, unarmed, just as Bolan was passing the control panel for the front doors. Without stopping, he punched the Close button. As he rolled out into the street, the doors clanged shut.

IT WAS a strange-looking crew that sat in the front room of the villa in the al-Murra compound at 4 a.m. Al-Murra and Turbah had practiced hoisting their mortars on slings over their backs. They were out of practice. The transport of mortar shells was another problem. They finally decided on only ten mortars to a team, strung around their waist on their webbing.

"Now that you've got that down, I've got some news for you," Bolan told them. "You'll have to make two trips."

"You've got to be kidding!" Grimaldi replied. "That makes us doubly vulnerable. Why?"

"I want a 60 mm with each team."

"You mean we've got to return to the street and haul up a 60 mm and ammo?" Turbah asked.

"Who feeds the belt-drive ammo for us?" al-Murra asked. "You'll have Grimaldi. We'll be alone."

"It'll feed itself if you lay it out carefully," Bolan said.

"We'll take a couple of my uncle's men. He has a few who've been trained in the national guard."

"You're not telling your uncle until it's all over, remember?"

"I've told him already. He wants to help."

Bolan turned his steely gaze on the man. He didn't care if Arabs took offense easily. Here was an SAS-trained man who'd forgotten his training. "I thought you knew how to follow orders," he said, his voice cold and controlled.

"I'm sorry," al-Murra said. "I had to tell my uncle. After all, this is his house."

"We're just three hours away from attack," Bolan said, his voice like a whip. "How many people did *he* tell?" The warrior couldn't remember when he'd been so angry. "How are we supposed to pull this off and get away?" This kind of unexpected exposure just confirmed his preference for working alone.

"My uncle is a man of honor. He hadn't told anyone, and he won't."

Bolan sighed wearily. "I trusted you."

"Come on, Mike. My uncle hasn't talked. Let me use two of his men to help. It'll be better. You'll see."

"All right," Bolan conceded. They had to get on with it. "This is your country, not mine. But it's my hide as well as yours. Jack and I won't just get a slap on the wrist if we get caught."

"Let's get the show on the road," Grimaldi suggested. "If our buddy told his uncle, we can't do anything now."

"No more discussion," Bolan said, motioning to al-Murra. "When we're finished here, you get your uncle's men and take off for your post. We each have a map. When we split up, it's every man for himself."

"I thought we were going to split up at the plane?"

"Change of plan, Adnan. Grimaldi and I take the Land Rover. You and Salman make your way back to your compound. Your uncle can take care of you."

"You're unhappy with me."

"Forget it. This is war."

"I can't part from you this way." The big Bedouin rose and came forward, his arms raised. He engulfed the warrior in a bear hug, then released him. "You're right. I've been a fool. But it's done. You're fighting my battle and I've endangered you. But you'll find that it's all right. We won't fail you."

He hugged Grimaldi before he slung his mortar over his shoulder. "My people are grateful, Jack."

Turbah rose from where he had squatted on the floor and hugged the two American warriors. "You are heroes. We will not forget you."

By the time they had finished their preparations it was almost six in the morning. Dawn was at seven. They picked up as much of their gear as they could and headed for the Land Rover.

"It's just you and me from now on, partner," Bolan said when they were alone. "If we see any false moves, we look out for ourselves."

"I'm with you, Striker. It's hit and git from now on, right?"

"Damned right."

CAPTAIN IBRAHIM SEDIK and Lieutenant Hassan Bindagii were released from the hospital after a day of intravenous saline treatment for the dehydration caused by their ordeal in the desert. They were flown back to Riyadh in a national guard hospital jet. The two men sat in Sedik's office, still burning over their capture by Bolan and the treatment he'd handed out.

"But he didn't kill us," Bindagii said.

"As far as I'm concerned, he intended to. If you hadn't been able to crawl to the knife. Well..."

"But he left the knife," Bindagii protested.

"Enough. We should be after him." Sedik overrode Bindagii's comment. "Remember the lies he was trying to get us to believe? They're our only clue now. We should head for Mecca and put him out of business once and for all.''

''But if he was telling the truth, he's working for us,'' Bindagii suggested.

''No one treats me as he did and lives. He's a dead man,'' Sedik growled. ''Get us a helicopter, an army gunboat this time, and don't take no for an answer.''

18

"We forgot the grenades," Grimaldi said as they struggled up the stairs with their load. Bolan had the mortar and the shells, Grimaldi the 60 mm gun.

"We couldn't use them. I should have realized earlier we'd be too far away from them to be effective."

"How long you figure it'll take you to set the charges?"

"Ten minutes. Less if I'm lucky," the Executioner replied, setting down the mortar on the flat gravel roof.

"Where are the others?" Grimaldi asked, looking over the low parapet of their roof.

Bolan pointed to two medium-size apartment buildings like their own. The team's positions formed a triangle with the Shiite compound laid out between, as vulnerable as a defenseless woman in the path of an invading army.

"You'd better get going," Grimaldi said. They were dressed in native clothes, the flowing ends of their *guttras* crossed over their faces like masks. The headdress had been designed for desert crossings and sandstorms, and they were ideal for concealment.

Bolan made it to the truck in two minutes, loaded himself down with explosives and snaked his way around the corner from the Land Rover to the front gate of the compound. The street was deserted, the sun just beginning to cast a faint glow of light above the buildings. He had the Beretta in his right hand, the silencer still in place.

The two sentries who had been indifferent suddenly sprang to life. They swung their SMGs toward the intruder but died within seconds of each other as a stream of 9 mm parabellums tore into their skulls, splashing gore against the pink-colored wall.

It wasn't quite light. Some of the Shiites, half-awake, stumbled around the compound, performing their morning ablutions. This was to be their big day. They had probably celebrated the night before. Bolan walked among them, his *guttra* covering his face. The wind cooperated by blowing dust from the compound's pavement, causing the others to cover their faces, as well.

Each house closely resembled the next: concrete blocks, pink stucco, an air conditioner jutting out beneath each window, a supply of propane piped in from the rear. The Executioner wasted no time. He circled the compound, molding a piece of C-4 and a detonator to each propane tank.

When he'd finished, Bolan raced back to the Land Rover, scooped up the box of belt ammunition and charged up the stairs. It didn't matter if anyone heard him now. All hell would break loose in a few minutes.

On the roof Grimaldi had everything laid out. "Ten minutes," he said.

Bolan looked at the scene below. A huge crowd, mostly men, were converging on the compound. They stopped and circled the block at a distance of about fifty feet.

"What's going on?" Grimaldi asked.

"Al-Murra," the big warrior replied. He'd uncovered his face, and his features were a study of granite. "So much for honor."

"They're going to get in the way."

"Too late. It's their problem now," Bolan said, working on the 60 mm. "When it hits the fan, they'd better get their butts out of there."

Grimaldi looked down at the compound and across at the other two installations. "Which is our sector?" he asked.

"The closest two houses and the open ground around them," Bolan replied as he fed belt ammo into the 60 mm that Grimaldi had set up on its tripod. He placed the ammo box so that the belt could feed freely.

"What's going down over there?" Grimaldi asked.

Bolan followed the pilot's pointing figure. Two Shiite men were examining the plastic explosive and were about to peel it from the pipe behind one of the buildings.

"We've got to move the action up," he yelled, reaching for the servomechanism.

He flipped a switch.

A red light glowed.

He pushed a button.

The compound erupted in five places at once, the noise washing toward them like a wave, battering their eardrums. It bounced off the mountains surrounding the city and came at them from the rear.

Chunks of concrete block and clouds of pink stucco flew in every direction. Blood and bone chips, mixed with the rest of the debris, pelted the survivors.

The mob fell to the ground and covered their ears, screaming for deliverance. The world had come to an end. Some of al-Murra's friends had been hit by large pieces of debris. Many fled, dragging the wounded with them. The wind carried pink and white plaster dust upward in swirling funnels, bringing with it the smell of death.

The other two teams hadn't wasted time. Though Bolan had fired almost ten minutes early, they went into action. Mortar shells pounded into the wreckage, pulverizing the piles of uneven rubble, spitting splinters of steel among the explosions, scything down the few who had escaped the first explosions and were running around in circles, dazed and disoriented, their eardrums ruptured, their world a silent hell.

The mortar barrage from the three rooftops took all of two minutes. Thirty explosions, all well placed, took down everything that had remained standing and flung pulverized flesh and bone in every direction. Only parts of the pink and green wall remained.

Even though Bolan and Grimaldi were busy trying to take out any survivors with the 60 mm, they could clearly see what the crowd of al-Murra men was doing. Many of them had grenades concealed beneath their robes and were running to the crumbling compound wall, despite the danger from multiple detonations inside, to toss the explosives into the rubble.

"Al-Murra's people!" Bolan shouted over the noise. "Guess we can't blame the old warrior. It's his fight more than ours."

"He's using the grenades we left behind."

The chatter of heavy weapon fire started up from the other roofs. A steady hail of fire raked the compound, kicking up small clouds of dust, rows of slugs hitting dirt, straight as a string, as they searched through the debris for targets.

Incredibly sporadic small-arms fire could be heard from below. An intermittent rain of 7.62 mm projectiles from scattered survivors arced upward to the other roofs. One of Bolan's allies on a distant roof took a slug in the chest. He stood, lost his footing, and pitched over the parapet. The white-robed body disappeared on the other side of the battlefield. A group of enemy soldiers escaped the wicked rain of death and disappeared into the street below Bolan's position.

Sirens could be heard over the battle sounds. Soon a wave of national guardsmen swarmed through the crowd, using their rifle butts as clubs. A struggle on one of the roofs on the other side of the compound ended with the death of two men, one of al-Murra's and a guardsman who had gained the roof as part of the first wave.

The Executioner and Grimaldi looked over the havoc they had wrought and headed for the stairs. Anything they could do now was overkill. If anyone survived in the Shiite compound, they wouldn't be able to muster a rebellion. The king was safe. The ayatollahs wouldn't make their objectives this year. It was time to get the hell out.

As they neared the stairs a group of three Rashidi warriors poured from the stairwell, their weapons spitting flame. Grimaldi went down.

Bolan fired his Beretta from the hip, hitting the first two men and driving them into the third. As the frustrated Rashidi tried to free himself of his wounded comrades, the thin man took a slug in the shoulder before a stream of 9 mm stingers lifted him off his feet and over the parapet. His scream trailed behind him as the other two tried to scramble to their feet.

Bolan treated them to another serving of lead and turned to his pilot. Grimaldi had taken one round in the thigh. His one good hand was trying to squeeze the flesh as blood poured from between his fingers. The Executioner moved quickly. Within seconds he had a tourniquet on the wound, swung his friend over his shoulder in a fireman's lift and headed down the stairs.

In a pall of smoke that swirled around the area carried by errant winds in the narrow canyons between the buildings, the two men weren't challenged by other guardsmen who were herding up bystanders and pushing them back. Hundreds of the military men, the national police of the kingdom, swarmed over the rubble of the ruined compound. In the confusion Bolan found their Land Rover. He placed his wounded companion in the back seat and took off, burning rubber.

The smell of death followed them as he forced a path between the thousands of curious pilgrims and the police who now filled the streets. For once he was lucky. The police were occupied with thousands of screaming pilgrims and were more concerned in keeping people out than throwing a cordon around the scene.

"Let's get out of here, Striker."

"No problem."

THE HELICOPTER FLEW LOW over the semidesert halfway between Zalim and Taif. The CID men would be over the latter city in a half hour.

"Don't worry, sir," Bindagii said. "If they headed for Mecca, we'll catch them."

"A message from your headquarters," the pilot said. "Someone has raided a compound within the Harram. All garrisons within two hundred miles are ordered to Mecca."

"It's them!" Captain Sedik shouted, smashing a fist into his palm. "We've got them!"

"But they told us we had enemies who would attack in Mecca," Bindagii said. "The attack could be the foreigner cleaning out the Shiites."

"You're a fool, Bindagii," Sedik said cruelly. "And that's why you'll never go farther in the service. We will capture them and we'll see them meet the ax. You'll see."

As they passed over Taif and the score of palaces perched on the side of the mountain, the pilot spoke again. "A small aircraft's taking off from a pesticide camp five miles to port. Could be the men you want, or it could be a routine pesticide flight. If it's the spraying crew, they wouldn't know about the raid on Mecca yet."

"Challenge them!" Sedik screamed.

The pilot swooped down the mountain face, picking up speed. The drop of a few thousand feet in a few seconds was second nature to him but not to his passengers. The pilot grinned at his navigator. They managed a second or two of eye contact and knew what the other was thinking—teach the arrogant bastard a lesson.

The drop had given the helicopter some added cruising speed. They caught the Cessna at two hundred feet as it banked to the right. They were less than a hundred feet from its starboard side.

"On your left! It's them!" Sedik screamed. "Order them down!"

The pilot flipped on his microphone and ordered the Cessna to land.

"They don't understand Arabic, you fool. Command them in English."

"If it's the men you want, they might have their radio off. They won't know our frequency and they wouldn't comply if they heard."

"Shoot them down!" Sedik ordered.

"I can't do that," the pilot replied.

"I order you to shoot them down!" Sedik continued to shout. He was beside himself. They were getting away. Already the Cessna had pulled ahead.

"This is a training aircraft, Captain," the pilot told him. "I was ordered to transport you to Mecca. We don't carry armament."

"What! This was supposed to be a gunship! Do *something*!" Sedik yelled. "They're heading for the sea."

The chopper pilot thumbed his microphone and called the base at Khamis Mashait. "Red Base. Red Base. This is Chopper T-247 from Blue Base."

"Roger, T-247. Got you loud and clear."

"The men responsible for the raid in Mecca believed to be in Cessna 172 heading for Jidda and the Red Sea," the pilot intoned casually. "Estimated altitude two hundred feet. Estimated speed three hundred kilometers per hour. Should cross the coast just south of Al-Kura. Do you copy?"

"Copy and out."

"What does that mean?" Sedik asked, sitting forward as much as his seat belt would permit.

"They'll send an alert to the base commander. If he agrees, they'll scramble a couple of F-16s."

"How long?" Sedik pressed, seeing his prey as a small dot in front of them.

"Not long. They respond quickly. Suppose we get out of the area?" the pilot suggested.

"I want to see this," Sedik protested.

"No way, Captain. Not unless you want a rocket up your ass." The pilot brought the chopper around in a turn to port. "We'll land you at the new airport at Jidda. You should be able to get land transport there."

"LOOKING GOOD," Bolan said, peeling off his *guttra* and robe while Grimaldi held the Cessna steady. He slipped into a shirt and slacks, trading his sandals for a pair of sneakers.

"Maybe," Grimaldi replied, taking his turn at changing while Bolan took the controls. "A whole search team will be after us in a few minutes." His new wound had stopped bleeding but was beginning to throb.

He kept the small plane close to the ground and crossed the coastline, heading for the Sudan. He knew that Bolan's operation had started in Khartoum. It was as good as destination as any.

The route was still a hundred miles across the Red Sea at that point. He'd been in worse spots and survived, but this was no picnic.

In minutes they were halfway across the sea, a beautiful dull green against the browns of both shores. Ahead, hundreds of dhows, the traditional cargo and fishing vessels of the Saudis for centuries, were strung out almost all the way to the Sudanese shore. The warriors were starting to feel confident when the first F-16 pulled alongside and tried to wave them back. Their airspeed was too slow for the jet. The Saudi pilot had difficulty holding his position and moved ahead.

Grimaldi flew lower, weaving from side to side, keeping a dhow beneath him as often as possible.

In one stretch, where the dhows were spread out, a rocket missed the small plane's wing tip by a few feet and exploded in front of them. The rush of water and concussion caught the plane's tail, slewing it around, sending them into a dangerous spin for a few seconds until Grimaldi had the aircraft under control.

The Sudanese coast loomed up and passed beneath them, the plane's shadow moving along the parched land, startling a few weary travelers, men and women looking for food, carrying their emaciated children, their dulled eyes searching the sky for the intruder.

They were safe. Unless the Sudanese scrambled their own ancient fighters, the soldiers were on their way home.

"I'm...starting...to lose it, Striker."

Bolan looked at his friend, concerned, and grabbed the controls. The terrain started to change from the low contours of the coastal plain. First a low ridge of hills forced Bolan to pull up to two thousand feet, then a mountain range blocked him. He had to take the small plane to a much higher ceiling. Grimaldi had passed out. His head lolled back and forth before it bumped into the portside window and rested against the Plexiglas.

No one had bothered Bolan for ten minutes or more. As far as he knew, the Saudi planes had peeled off over the coast.

Bolan's peripheral vision picked up something next to his port wing tip—a vintage Phantom jet fighter was tracking them, signaling them to land or be fired on. He was in as much trouble with an old jet as with the ultramodern F-16. Against either, in the eggshell skin of the Cessna, they were dead.

Bolan scanned the sky ahead, saw a Saudi F-16 circling to come in behind and cursed. So the bastards hadn't given up. This was big trouble. He could hear

Sudanese control shouting at the Saudis in English, angrily ordering them to clear their airspace. The Saudis refused to budge and lined up behind the Cessna for an attack.

Bolan searched the sky. He could see a Phantom above and behind him. A Saudi F-16 was still on his tail.

The unmistakable blast of a rocket leaving a wing cradle turned his blood to ice, and he pulled the control toward him, taking the aircraft up into a stall. Behind him the sky mushroomed into a fiery ball of orange and red. The heat-seeking rocket had zeroed in on the more powerful Phantom power plant.

The Saudi pilot had hit a Phantom!

They were still coming on. Bolan was at stall speed, nose up. Khartoum was just ahead. A rocket flashed past his wing tip, then suddenly a Phantom came out of nowhere and downed the F-16. Its fiery cloud of debris fell on the Sudanese countryside not far from the city.

They were alone in the sky with the remaining jet. The African pilot would be flushed with victory. Two kills painted on his fuselage would be better than one. Few would know that the second kill was a defenseless Cessna.

The Phantom toyed with them as they made their approach into Khartoum, firing strings of cannon shells past their nose. They continued to make their approach, Bolan gripping the wheel until his knuckles were white, jaw clamped tight.

At the last minute, the Phantom shot away their landing gear. Bolan pulled up and circled the field. The Sudanese pulled alongside, grinned wickedly, enjoying the game. Then, wagging his wings in a salute, he peeled off head to his base.

Grimaldi came around, shook his head and took in the scene. He grabbed for the controls and had the Cessna back in position in seconds.

They were alone in the sky, trapped in the thin skin of a lethal vehicle. Without landing gear they could end up just as dead as if a rocket had blown them out of the sky.

Grimaldi thumbed the KX170B. "Khartoum, this is Cessna SA540. We've got a small problem here."

"Roger, SA540. We've had you on radar and visual. Our crew is laying down a foam skid path now. Runway Two. You should be able to see them."

"We're down to ten minutes of fuel," Grimaldi advised.

"Hold on as long as you can," the nasal sound came through on a poor connection. "Takes a little longer than that."

"Don't have longer than that," Grimaldi grumbled to himself as he tapped the fuel gauge with his finger. The needle dropped even farther. It had been on empty. Now it rested on the lowest limit pin, below empty. The engine coughed, then settled down to a steady hum again.

Grimaldi punched the microphone button. "That's it," he announced. "Get your men out of the way. We're coming in, *now*."

He banked to port, lined up on the runway and nosed her down slowly. "I've put one of these things down in less than a hundred feet," he told his friend without taking his eyes from the runway.

"Without wheels?" Bolan asked.

"Never tried it without wheels. Maybe we can beat my old record."

The fuselage touched the slippery foam, slippery being the general idea. The foam would prevent sparks and without sparks there was no fire.

They ran out of foamed runway. The light aluminum skin started to disintegrate as the drag of the asphalt caught the underbelly. One wing dipped and churned up grass from the verge, then the Cessna slewed around and started to break up. Just when Grimaldi expected the aircraft to cartwheel and rip into shreds, it skidded all the way onto the verge and a patch of marshy grassland.

The stop was abrupt, pulling on their seat belts and tugging at their guts. Grimaldi's thigh squirted blood on the windshield.

"Get the hell out!" he yelled, trying to stem the flow.

They unhooked and jumped to the ground from different sides. Grimaldi hobbled away as fast as he could. They met fifty feet from the shattered hulk just as she blew. The concussion knocked them down.

Bolan picked himself up and pulled Grimaldi by his good arm until they were safely out of the intense heat.

Grimaldi started to laugh as he sat on the runway, holding his throbbing leg. "She held together for us," he said, looking up at his friend. "Not enough fuel left to really blow us to eternity though," he continued. He was almost out of it, the laugh closer to hysteria than humor. "Seems to me you promised a celebration after this," he said, relief evident in his face. "Bring on the dancing girls."

Phoenix Force—bonded in secrecy to avenge the acts of terrorists everywhere.

Super Phoenix Force #2

American "killer" mercenaries are involved in a KGB plot to overthrow the government of a South Pacific island. The American President, anxious to preserve his country's image and not disturb the precarious position of the island nation's government, sends in the experts—Phoenix Force—to prevent a coup.